A Vampire Wedding

A Novella
Bitten by Love #4

Stacy McKitrick

MYTHICAL PRESS * DAYTON, OHIO

MYTHICAL PRESS * DAYTON, OHIO
www.mythicalpress.com

Cover designed by JMick Consulting, LLC

Edited by Paige Christian and Stephanie McKitrick

Formatted by Enterprise Book Services
http://www.EnterpriseBookServices.com/

Print ISBN: 978-0-9967976-3-4

Books by Stacy McKitrick

Bitten by Love Series

My Sunny Vampire (Book #1)

Bite Me, I'm Yours (Book #2)

Blind Temptation (Book #3)

Ghostly Encounters Series

Ghostly Liaison (Book #1)

Short Stories in the Following Anthologies

Home for the Holidays

Love's a Beach

ACKNOWLEDGMENTS

I'd like to think my stories are fine without editors, and maybe they are, but they definitely don't shine. Thank you, Paige Christian, for pointing out the weaknesses I was sure were there but couldn't see. And thank you, Stephanie McKitrick, for finding all the nit-picky stuff. You two are the best editors a writer could ever hope for.

Thanks to Fotolia, I was able to find the almost perfect picture for the cover. And thanks to JMick Consulting, LLC for making it perfect. You are awesome!

Thanks to Kim H. and Robin M. for beta reading. It's much appreciated. You gave me the confidence I needed that this novella was ready for the public.

Thanks to Enterprise Book Services for getting this formatted quickly and beautifully. I couldn't have published this without your help.

Finally, thanks to my husband, Jim. Your support means more than you'll ever know.

DEDICATION

To all the readers who love John and Sarah as much
as I do

Chapter 1

What was the point in being immortal if you could still feel ill?

Sitting in the breakfast nook of John's Urbana home, Sarah stabbed the eggs on her plate, but didn't raise the fork to her mouth. If she took another bite, it just might come back up.

Her upset stomach had nothing to do with a disease—she probably couldn't even get one of those anymore—and it certainly wasn't the result of the wonderful breakfast John had prepared for her. No, this sick feeling came from one source and one source only.

She glanced at her cell phone situated above her plate.

How the hell did she get my number? And how many more times would she call?

John looked up from the laptop he'd brought over to the kitchen table. "What's wrong? Too much salt? Not enough?"

He would blame himself for her not eating. Sarah forced a smile. "Nothing's wrong with it. It's great."

"Then what's the matter? You said you'd eat if we were alone. And I'm not watching."

Technically, she'd said she'd eat if *she* were alone or with other mortals. She still had difficulty eating in front of him when he couldn't enjoy the meal. Then he'd discovered if he went to the trouble of preparing her food—and for a vampire, he sure knew how to cook—she'd feel guiltier not eating it. And she'd be eating now if only she hadn't gotten that call. After everything that had happened in the last few months, that one person shouldn't affect her anymore. So why did she? "Just feeling a little…hormonal."

The lie tasted bitter on her tongue, but the truth would be more distasteful.

"Hormonal? You haven't felt like that since the bonding, have you?"

She shook her head. One lie was enough. It was no secret to John that her cycles were erratic. Had been since the day Steven had pushed her down the stairs, causing her to lose the baby and ruining any chance of another pregnancy. After she'd completed the bond with John and became immortal—or so everyone believed—her scars had faded, so it only made sense that her insides had been fixed, too. But no such luck. The calendar was still useless to her.

"Well, try to eat something. Maybe it will help." He returned to reading whatever had captured his attention. Or he was doing a good job of acting like something was interesting on that laptop. He did his best to make her feel at ease eating around him, but even if he left her alone now, it wouldn't matter.

If only she *were* hormonal. But she would try

eating. As she brought the fork to her mouth, her cell phone rang again. Damn it. Her heart sank, along with her hand, food uneaten.

Go away, go away, go away!

"You gonna get that?" John asked.

"It's a wrong number." The lies were coming easier, weren't they? She moved the phone out of his reach, in case he decided to answer it. Because it wasn't a wrong number. No, of course not. But talking to that devil woman was not an option. Was she supposed to ignore the fact she'd heard no word in over a year? Pain radiated in her chest and her eyes stung from threatening tears. Damn. She would not cry. Would. Not. That was the old Sarah. The new, improved version didn't cry.

"You sure?"

The phone stopped ringing. Sarah breathed in relief. Maybe now she'd have some peace. "Yes, I'm sure. She called earlier and I told her so. I guess some people are just idiots."

The phone chimed.

And she was a colossal idiot to think it would ever end. Sarah had never gotten the last word in and it seemed she wouldn't this time either.

John peered around his laptop. "Do wrong numbers usually leave a message?"

Not usually, did they? Damn it. She really didn't want to get into this, but now what choice did she have? Little lies were one thing. After a heavy sigh, she slid the phone over to John—with a nod to have at it—then stood and carried her half-eaten breakfast into the kitchen. No way could she eat it now.

While she rinsed the egg and potatoes down the drain, he listened to the message. His head jerked up and he stared at her. "It's your mother? I thought she was dead."

Now there was a thought. "Why would you think that?"

"Because you never talked about her. Not once. Why'd you say it was a wrong number?"

"To me she is a wrong number. It's hard to talk about someone who's turned against you."

"I find that hard to believe, Sarah. She's your mother."

She grabbed a towel and dried her hands. "Just because your mother was perfect doesn't mean they all are."

He came over to her and leaned against the counter. "Does this mean your father is alive?"

"Yes. He's alive."

"Are you avoiding him, too?"

"No. I call him when he's at work. It's the safest time to talk. Sometimes I wish he'd just divorce Mom so I could go see him, but for some strange reason he won't leave her."

"Because he loves her."

"I suppose." Or he was too scared to be alone. Sarah had felt the same way until Steven pushed her down the stairs. That wake-up call had cost her dearly.

"This does bring up something you need to think about. When it comes time for us to move on and let people think we died, is this how you want to leave your parents?"

"We have to die?" She knew she would have to quit her job and disappear, but dead? "Why?"

"Because we won't age. We've gone over this."

"I know, I know. I just didn't think that far in

advance." Or at all, really. He assumed she wouldn't age and maybe she wouldn't. When they bonded, she hadn't become a vampire like John. She still ate regular food and enjoyed the sun. John called them perks; she called them normal. Being immortal would be a definite bonus, but it was still only a theory and not something she wished to dwell upon. She healed quickly and had survived a mortal wound, making her hard to kill—a valid "perk" if she went there—so hopefully she'd age just like him: not at all.

"So you'll call your mother back? Maybe tell her you're engaged?"

Anger shot the words out of her mouth before she could stop them. "Hell no!"

"Sweetie, I understand you had a falling out, but she's your mother. Aren't you even curious what she wants?"

"Falling out? Is that what you think?"

"I don't know what to think. You've never told me anything."

She lowered her head and toyed with the bottom of her shirt. Of course she'd never told him anything. Who wanted to admit their mother was a horrid person? But maybe it was time to spill. He'd never drop it otherwise. "She thinks Steven had every right to abuse me."

"She didn't say that." He paused for a beat of a second. "Did she?"

"Ever since the day she met him, she's taken his side. I was just too blind to see it at the time. I had made her happy. I'd never done that before and I wasn't going to question it. But when Steven started to abuse me, I went to her and asked for advice. And what does she tell me? That Dad and Grandma had spoiled me, that I was selfish, and that Steven had every right to *correct* me. To be glad I'd married someone strong instead of weak like she had." Her heart ached at the memory, but her eyes remained dry. She had no more tears on this subject.

John bent down and lifted her chin with his finger. His eyes were full of compassion. "I can only imagine the pain you must have felt. But don't you think it's possible she called to apologize? Steven is in jail. She must know that."

She'd like to hope that's why her mother had called, but she'd had her hope crushed too many times to go that route. "Is that what she said in the message?"

"Well. No. She just asked for you to return her call."

"See?"

John rubbed his thumb over her cheek and she leaned into it. She'd love to talk about something else. Anything else. Better yet, not even talk.

"Maybe she has news concerning your father. That's not something you leave in a message."

"Oh." Her heart stung at the possibility that something might have happened to her father. "Fine. I'll call. Now will you drop it?"

He shook his head. "I would like you to invite them over. I don't think the first meet should be at our wedding, do you?"

Ah crap. This was not how she'd meant to bring up the subject. It still amazed her that he wanted to marry her. What was the point in making it official if they would eventually be declared dead? But he wanted that piece of paper and she would oblige. Just not with all the pomp and circumstance.

She lowered her head and looked at the floor. "Well, about that. I was hoping we could elope and I wouldn't have to invite anyone." She wrung her hands. "You didn't want a big wedding, did you?"

* * * *

Elope?

John stared at the love of his life. Sure, he didn't have a lot of friends and his family was long dead, but he'd never dreamed they would elope.

Sarah wrapped her arms around him. "I'm sorry, John. I just want our wedding to be fun. Big weddings are more stressful."

"I understand that, and I wasn't expecting anything fancy, but wouldn't you have more fun with your friends and family there? I know I would. But if you're hell-bent on eloping…"

She covered his lips with her fingers. "I'm not hell-bent on anything. I just assumed… I mean, most guys just want to be told when and where."

"In case you haven't noticed, I'm not most guys." Eloping seemed so sneaky. Like he had to hide her.

"You've thought about our wedding?"

"Sure. Just because I'm a vampire doesn't mean I don't want to show you off." And to announce to every vampire that she belonged to him and only him.

Completing the bond had done the same thing. While he remained affected, her scent no longer drew another vampire's attention, and if they touched her, they wouldn't feel the rush of warmth. But could another vampire break their bond? That was a major concern among the Perfect Mate couples, and he really didn't want to be the one to find out.

Okay, maybe she had something with this smaller wedding thing. Didn't mean he wanted to elope.

"What kind of wedding did you think we'd have?" she asked.

He led her into the family room and settled onto the couch with her on his lap. His favorite sitting position. It aligned her lips perfectly and, as usual, he couldn't resist a taste. He would never grow tired of kissing her.

She broke the kiss, breathless. "You keep this up and we'll never plan our wedding."

He chuckled while nuzzling her neck. Her strawberry scent came alive and he grew hard. And hungry. There'd been a time he would have resisted the hunger part, but now that he knew he couldn't hurt her... "Is that what we're doing?"

"I thought so, but this is nice too."

"Just nice?" He licked her neck and she tensed in his arms, waiting for the bite. And while he'd love nothing better than to taste her, they should probably resolve their wedding arrangements first. He didn't mind torturing her, though. "Then I guess I'll stop."

"You're such a tease, John Pennington."

"No, just a preview of what's to come."

"I'm going to hold you to that." She turned and straddled his lap, facing him. "So tell me what kind of wedding you want."

"I thought we'd get married outside, at night of course, on the rooftop of Wings. Followed by a reception. Nothing fancy. Just our friends." He brought his face close to hers. "And relatives."

"Oh? And what relatives of yours are coming? Huh?"

"Very funny. Are you going to invite them or not?" Sure, families could get into some squabbles, but she would regret not inviting them eventually.

Especially when the time came to move.

She sighed. "How about a compromise?"

"Go on. I'm listening."

"I'm okay with the small wedding, but I'd like to have it somewhere else. Like maybe…Vegas."

"Vegas?" That would require flying. No way would she want to drive that far.

"Please? The Mighty Grand has chapels. And I won't have to do much work. Most of all, it'll be fun."

"You don't have to do any work if you don't want to. I can do it."

"I know that, but wouldn't you prefer to go someplace where you don't have to go outside? It's all indoors. Not a window in sight. Well, except for the hotel room, but they have blinds."

"You've done some research."

"A little."

More like a lot. "Will you invite your parents?"

She rested her head on his shoulder. "Not Mom. I'll invite Dad and Grandma, and of course Lori, but not Mom. I'll not have her spoil our day."

Maybe her attitude would change once she talked to her mother. Until then he'd do everything in his power to make her happy. "I can do Vegas."

"Oh, John!" She hugged him tight and kissed him. "Thank you. I love you so much."

No more than he loved her. "So, did you pick a date, too?"

She climbed off his lap and headed for the laptop. "Let's go see what's available."

In a matter of moments she reached the site. Seemed June 28 was open. Less than a month. He couldn't wait. Now to finish what he'd started earlier.

He scooped her into his arms and climbed the

stairs.

She ran a finger down his cheek and ended at his lips. "Breakfast time for you?"

"Among other things." He lowered his fangs and flashed them, bringing a huge smile to her face.

Since their bond, he actually enjoyed being a vampire. If only there were more Perfect Mates out there for other vampires, then maybe he wouldn't worry so much.

But she was rare. And he would worry.

Chapter 2

"Hey, how was Atlanta? Do anything fun?"

Sarah was facing away from her office door and jumped at her friend's questions. When she turned, the sight caught her off guard. Lori usually wore flowing tops and short skirts with bright colors, not a conservative-looking, navy blue pantsuit.

"What's with the outfit? Got an interview or something?" That was usually the joke around the office whenever anyone dressed up.

Lori entered, looked down at her outfit as if she'd forgotten what she wore, and then picked a piece of lint off her lapel. "Apparently I overdid it with the wardrobe Friday, and I got a little chewed out. Figured I'd be good for a while." She sat in the chair in front of Sarah's desk and crossed her legs. "So, Atlanta? Fun?"

Sarah couldn't say that she and John had gone to Atlanta for the June Committee meeting. Like all mortals, Lori had no idea vampires even existed. "It was a business trip for John. I just went along for the ride. We did pick a wedding date, though. How's June 28th? In Vegas?"

Ah, the misdirection worked. Lori's eyes widened. "Vegas? Hot damn. I'm in. But will you get everything done before then?"

"It shouldn't take long because we're not doing anything elaborate. If I have my way, we'll wear jeans. I want this wedding to be fun."

"When you marry the right guy, the wedding is fun. Are you inviting your folks?" Sarah's desk phone rang. Lori looked up at the clock and grimaced. "Oh shit. You didn't see me. We'll talk at lunch, okay?"

She zipped out of the office. Maybe she'd been chewed out for more than her wardrobe. Just as well she had to leave. Sarah certainly didn't want to talk about her family at work.

The phone call ended up being a client instead of the boss and thus began a busy morning without another thought of her mother. By the time Lori appeared for lunch, Sarah was ready for the break.

"I'll drive, okay?" Lori said.

"You don't want to eat in town?" During the summer they usually walked somewhere. And by the looks of the blue sky, the day was turning out to be a rather nice one. She never could walk in the sun with John.

"Don't want to run into anyone from here."

That seemed fair enough, especially if she was avoiding the person who had chewed her out. But instead of driving to a sit-down restaurant, or even a regular fast-food joint, Lori pulled into a drive-in.

"Why are we here?" It was unlike Lori to go someplace where she couldn't ogle the waiters.

"Thought it would give us more privacy to talk."

Ah crap. That meant Lori wanted to talk about Sarah's family. Not a subject that would stimulate an appetite.

Lori rolled down her window and pushed the order button. She chose the grilled chicken sandwich meal and Sarah chose the double cheeseburger and large order of onion rings. Having her big meal for lunch—out of John's eyesight—made it easier to eat a salad for dinner in his presence. Who drooled over lettuce?

But lately her appetite had been nonexistent. Was it possible the bond was making her more vampire than human? When John had fed from her yesterday, she'd gotten a sudden urge to bite him. Problem was, biting a vampire wasn't a vampire trait. If it weren't for the fact her paper cuts healed in record time, and they could still communicate telepathically, she'd suspect she needed more of his blood to maintain their bond. So until she exhibited more unusual traits, she'd keep that biting urge a secret. Why worry him needlessly?

"With the way you've been eating at lunch, I'd assume you'd be as big as a blimp by now. It's not fair. I just look at fried food and gain five pounds. What's your secret? Or is John keeping you from eating dinner?"

"I eat dinner. I found eating my large meal at lunch is healthier." Explaining her food hang-up to Lori would only garner more questions. Besides, her Perfect Mate status actually attributed to her new body image. She might have lost a few inches here and there, but she'd gained a few pounds. No excess body fat on her, no siree. Okay, guess she could add another perk to being a bonded Perfect Mate.

"You call eating onion rings healthy?"

"I said health*ier*." And this was why Sarah hated lying. It never turned out the way she wanted. "Why are we eating in the car? You afraid I'll cuss or something?"

"Cuss? Oh, your mother." Lori drummed her fingers on the steering wheel. "I mean, I wanted to talk without anyone overhearing us, but not about your mother." She giggled. "I think I'm in love."

In love? Sarah stared at her friend. Had she been so wrapped up in John that she hadn't noticed Lori was dating someone regularly? "With who?"

"His name is Kyle Hennessey and he's no one you know. He lives in my apartment complex and I ran into him Friday. Well, actually, we ran into each other—literally." Lori sighed and stared out the front window as if she were reliving the day.

"You're in love with someone you just met on Friday?"

Lori turned Sarah's way, her expression practically glowing. "I know. Crazy, huh? But you know how it is. Didn't you pretty much fall in love with John when you first met him?"

"No." More like the first time they touched, but why encourage Lori with the facts? Kyle wasn't a vampire. Was he?

"Okay, so not the first time, but close enough. I saw how you acted after that disastrous first date."

"That was different," Sarah muttered. John hadn't known Perfect Mates existed and the connection between them, along with his inability to read her mind, had scared him.

Lori frowned. "Oh, so what you're saying is it's

okay for you to fall in love at first sight, but not okay for me?"

"And if I recall correctly, you lambasted me for falling so fast and hard for John. Have you slept with Kyle already?" Sarah regretted the question as soon as it left her mouth. What did it matter? If Lori was in love, who was she to knock her down?

Lori turned her head away. "Out of everyone I know, I was sure you'd understand. My sisters laughed at me when I told them about Kyle." She looked down at her hands and murmured, "Am I really that promiscuous?"

"No, of course not." Lori was her best friend and she wouldn't hurt her for the world. "I'm sorry. Maybe you do love him. Who am I to say you don't? So how is Kyle different from say…Perry?" When Lori had dated John's vampire friend, she had claimed it was purely for the sex. For both of them. Except that last bit wasn't true. He'd gotten a meal out of their encounter, too.

Sarah had hated Perry for that—because there was no way Lori could have given permission—but eventually forgave him. Kind of had to since he was going to be John's best man. Plus, Lori had seemed unaffected.

Lori's eyes brimmed with tears. "Kyle is nothing like Perry. He's more like John. Perry can be a little self-indulgent."

"Only a little?"

Lori laughed and wiped her hand across her eyes, smearing her mascara. "No. More like a lot. But Kyle…he cares about me. No one's ever treated me like a lady before. I don't want to lose that."

Sarah reached into her purse and took out a tissue.

When she handed it to Lori, Lori lowered the visor and assessed the damage.

"No one says you have to lose that," Sarah said. "But I wouldn't go declaring your love until you've known him a little longer. You don't want to scare the poor guy away."

The server chose that opportunity to skate over with their order. Once Lori divvied up the food, she said, "You're right. Maybe it isn't love, but whatever it is, I don't want it to go away. I've never felt this way before. I don't want to screw it up."

"Then do what you told me to do. Take it slow. If he's for real, he won't rush things." Sarah unwrapped the double cheeseburger and her jaw dropped. The burger was huge.

"How the hell are you going to eat that?" Lori asked while unwrapping her chicken sandwich.

Good question. The thing looked larger than Sarah's mouth. Crap. There wasn't any way she could eat it, not without removing something. She pulled out one of the meat patties. The lettuce and tomato came loose and landed in her lap.

Lori nearly spit out her food, laughing. "Geez, Sarah. I can't take you anywhere, can I?"

Sarah snickered. "This wouldn't be happening if we ate in a restaurant instead of a car." Normally she would cut her burger. "Now shut up and hand me a napkin." Still laughing, Lori dangled a napkin in front of Sarah's face. Sarah snatched it from her friend's grasp.

As Sarah picked up the remnants of her sandwich, Lori said, "For the record, I didn't sleep with him. He hasn't even made any moves on me yet." Her eyes got big. "God, you don't think he's gay, do you?"

"Why do you automatically go there? If he's gay, do you really think he would have asked you out?"

Lori paused in thought for a micro-second. "Good point."

They ate in silence for a bit, or more accurately, Lori ate in silence. After two bites, Sarah could only stare at her meal. The burger was way too much for her. Somewhere along the way her stomach must have shrunk.

"Hey, can I bring him to the wedding?"

What him? Oh, Kyle. "You do know Perry will be there."

"He will?"

"He's John's best man."

"When did they make up?"

How did Lori know they'd been fighting? "What do you know about that?"

Lori shrugged. "He mentioned a falling out."

"When? They fought after your date."

"Yeah, the first date, but I've been seeing him about once a month now."

"What? And you're just now telling me this?"

"I didn't think you were interested in my sex life. And, plus, he asked me not to."

"Of course he did." Oh God. Sarah rubbed her stomach. The few bites she'd managed to get down sat in her stomach like an anvil. There was no way Perry was only dating Lori for sex. And to think she'd forgiven him.

"It doesn't matter anyway. It's over between us."

"Don't you think it would be weird then, to have Kyle and Perry in the same room?"

"No. I never loved Perry and I know he doesn't love me. Don't get me wrong. He's a great guy, but

I'm not the woman for him. I can tell. Doesn't mean we couldn't have fun. But he's the past. Kyle's my present and hopefully future. So, can I bring him?"

Maybe what Lori said was true, but if she had fallen for Perry, he could have easily made her forget. That man had no morals. As for him falling in love? Lori had gotten that one right. He didn't know the meaning of the word.

"If Kyle wants to fly out to Vegas with you, I don't see why not. It's not like I'm going to have family there." And she had her mother to thank for that. She'd returned the call, shared the news about getting married, and had gotten scolded in the process. Scolded! As if she were still a child under that woman's thumb. Thank goodness John had witnessed that debacle of a phone conversation. He'd promised never to mention her mother again.

"Uh-oh. What happened?"

She wrapped up her burger. No way could she eat it now. Even the onion rings smelled unappealing and they were her favorite. "My mother is what happened. She still thinks I should be with Steven."

"What? Doesn't she know he's in jail for what he did to you?"

"She knows. Blames me for that, too."

Lori grabbed Sarah's shoulder. "I never thought I'd say this, but your mother is a whack job. She doesn't deserve an awesome daughter like you."

Sarah stuffed the burger in the bag with the onion rings. "Thanks. John pretty much said the same thing."

"I knew he was a smart man." Lori pointed to the bag. "Aren't you going to eat that?"

"I lost my appetite."

"Ah, cheer up. You didn't want her at your wedding anyway."

"No, but I wanted Dad there. He said if he came, he couldn't guarantee she wouldn't follow. And it would be like her to spoil it for me. He thinks it would be best if he keeps an eye on her. I don't know why he stays with her."

"Maybe he stays with her to protect you."

Somehow that didn't dull the ache in her heart.

Chapter 3

Riding in the backseat of his Xterra during daylight hours turned out better than John had expected. Sure, each inadvertent hit of the sun drained him a bit—probably about as much as having sex did—but he no longer felt the instant sting of burning skin.

Was Sarah's blood protecting him? Next time he spoke with Victoria, one of the Committee members who was also bonded to a Perfect Mate, he'd ask. But telling Barnet, the head of the Committee, was out of the question for now. John respected the man, but he tended to get a little over-enthusiastic whenever a new Perfect Mate trait emerged.

Sarah turned left into the parking lot of an apartment complex. Seemed unfair she had to drive the whole way—he'd suggested the trip—but he'd be able to drive home since it would be dark by then.

When Sarah's grandmother informed them that she couldn't make it out to their wedding, Sarah had been disheartened. Now none of her family was coming. He blamed himself for her misery. If he'd just left it alone, they'd have the same result, but Sarah wouldn't be hurt. So to cheer her up, John had suggested they visit her grandmother. They'd be visiting her father, too, but no one wanted her mother to find out. Seemed Sarah wasn't the only one avoiding the woman.

Shade surrounded them as she pulled up to the building. She turned around in the seat and frowned. "You're pale."

"I'm always pale."

She shook her head. "More than usual. The backseat might have kept you from burning, but it wasn't one hundred percent effective. Here, take some blood."

With her arm proffered before him, his fangs extended, among other things. Appeared he didn't need a taste to get a hard-on. He shifted in the seat. "If I take your blood, then I'll only get us horny."

Or just her, since he was already there. That little side effect was wonderful in bed. Out in public? Not so much.

"I can live with being horny. I don't want you to end up paralyzed on the floor."

She had a point. Just because his skin hadn't burned didn't mean he wasn't affected. Being paralyzed hadn't been pleasant, and at the time he had refused to take her blood because he'd been sure he'd lose control and take too much. If he'd known the bond he'd started would have prevented that, he might have acted differently. "Fine, but not here. Go someplace shady and private."

After she parked behind some kind of maintenance building, he figured she'd stick her arm between the seats again and he'd have at it. Instead she climbed out of the SUV.

"Where are you—" Before he could finish, she climbed into the back seat with him.

Her smile practically glowed. "If we're gonna hide, might as well take advantage of getting horny. Besides, I've never done it in a car before. Knew there was a reason to wear a dress today."

And it was a very pretty dress. Looked like sunshine with the yellow and orange. But what she suggested… "You want to do it—" He shook his head. "No."

"Why not? No one's gonna see us." She proceeded to remove her panties. The light pink panties. She probably wore the matching bra, too.

His dick jerked as if asking, "You gonna just sit there?" Oh hell no. In no time he freed his erection and slid his pants under his butt. If she wasn't worried about being seen, why should he?

She'd told him many times that she was a sex junkie when it came to him. Guess if she had to be hooked on something, at least it was him. He was certainly hooked on her.

As she straddled him, he tugged on the neckline of her dress and peeked. Oh yeah. The pink bra.

* * * *

Thinking about John biting her made Sarah wet for him. Should she feel bad that she was glad he needed her blood? Probably a blessing he never needed that much or she could kiss these spontaneous love sessions goodbye. If he even got a hint that he harmed her in any way, he'd put a stop to it. Even now, if he knew her stomach had been a bit on the fritz, he might have stopped, but once she got a whiff of his scent, her stomach calmed and her heart raced.

She impaled herself on his ever-ready erection. All sweet heat and electrifying thrill came over her from their shared experience. She bared her neck. "I'm all yours."

"Yes, you are." He cupped her face and thoroughly kissed her, their tongues dancing together. She nipped at his bottom lip when he moved to nuzzle her neck.

The bite came quick and she nearly orgasmed on the spot. A sweet, coppery flavor filled her mouth. Ambrosia. Or at least John thought so. He loved the taste of her and, with their shared experience, she did, too.

That urge to bite him back came over her. Stronger than the last time. Was her body telling her something or was it a residual effect from his bite? Maybe one day she'd find out, but today wasn't that day.

Sooner than she liked, he licked her neck, but when he kissed her again, she got another taste of her blood and practically sucked the remnants from his mouth. For not being a vampire, she sure loved the flavor. Guess that was part of being his Perfect Mate.

He held her hips and pounded into her. Whenever he took her blood he usually prolonged the lovemaking, but since they were in the backseat of the Bumblebee, in the middle of the day, he probably wanted to end this sooner rather than later.

Ahh, the price of doing it in the car during daylight. But man, what a rush.

Her release came simultaneously with his and she collapsed onto his chest. Being in his arms was better than any bed, and she was willing to stay there for a while longer, but movement out the back window caught her attention. "Uh-oh. Someone's coming."

She reached for the tissue box on the floorboard while John chuckled. "No one's gonna see, huh?"

"Oh shut up. You had fun. Besides, you can get rid of him."

"Not with the windows up."

She'd forgotten. Not that they'd ever run into that problem before. After cleaning the best she could, and leaving her panties behind, she climbed out of the SUV, hoping the man couldn't see through her dress.

Moot point. As soon as she'd opened the door, John had taken control of the older gentleman. With robotic movements, the man made an about-face and walked back the way he'd come. She knew better than to say anything. It was a sore subject for John; he hated how he couldn't control people smoothly like other vampires could.

Instead, she grinned at him and said, "My hero."

Shaking his head, he threw her panties at her. She could only laugh.

* * * *

Standing in the hallway, John checked his shirt and jeans again. He couldn't deny that her blood was a welcome boost, but he would have preferred not looking...satiated. Sexually.

"You're fine," Sarah said.

"I wanted to make a good impression and not look like I had...you know."

She giggled. "Well, you made a good impression on me. Relax."

The door opened and the scent of meat cooking filled the air. An elderly woman wearing a flowery top and light blue polyester pants stood in the doorway.

"Grandma!" Sarah ran into her grandmother's arms and wrapped her in a hug. "It's so good to see you."

"Oh, Sarah. It's been too long. I'm so glad you could come over." When she stepped back and looked at John, she placed her hand on her chest. "Oh my."

"Grandma, this is my fiancé, John Pennington. John, this is my grandmother, Marie Simpson."

John held his hand out. "How do you do, Mrs. Simpson?"

"Please, call me Marie." She looked him up and down. "John Pennington, huh? That makes sense. I thought you looked familiar."

"You know me?" He hadn't bothered reading her mind when they shook hands and now he wished he had. Maybe she'd visited Wings, his bar. Though, if he'd seen her, he would have remembered.

"No, but I knew someone who looked just like you. Most likely your grandfather. You really are the spitting image of him. Oh, where are my manners? Come on in. Let's talk where it's more comfortable."

Grandfather? Shit. Had she been a patient? He'd delivered a lot of babies in Columbus back in the fifties, but couldn't remember any patient named Simpson, not that he could recall them all. He'd been mortal at the time and his memory of those days was fuzzier than since he'd been turned. Who was this woman and how did she know him?

As he entered the apartment, Sarah turned and gave him a questioning look. He could only shrug.

Marie ushered them into the living room and played the polite hostess by gathering drink orders.

John sat beside Sarah on the couch and took her hand to calm his nerves.

"Relax, John," Sarah said through their link. *"She doesn't know you're the same person, but I think it's rather interesting that she knew you. Do you remember her?"*

"Name doesn't sound familiar." And she was right. There was no way Marie would suspect he was the same John Pennington she'd known. But still… It was freaky. What were the odds? Astronomical, that's what.

Marie returned with a pitcher of iced tea and placed it on the coffee table.

Sarah turned toward her grandmother. "How did you know John's grandfather?"

"I used to date him." Marie sat in a chair and poured tea into a glass.

"Date him?" Sarah raised her eyebrows as she took the glass.

John pictured Marie without wrinkles and with brunette hair instead of white. Oh shit. Could it be? *"I dated a Marie Collier in high school."*

"That would be her, then."

Marie filled another glass and offered it to John, but he waved it away. "Yes, date him. I did date before I got married, you know."

Sarah laughed. "Sorry. I just didn't know you grew up in Urbana."

"Lived there until I married your grandfather. His job brought us to Cambridge." She studied him some more while she took a drink. "I can't believe how much you look like him."

Her scrutiny made John squirm. Sure, he could make her change the subject, but that would be rude and Sarah wouldn't approve. He smiled instead. "Do

I? He died before I was born."

"Yes, I suppose he had. I heard he'd gone missing. To think I might have been married to him if I hadn't met your grandfather."

"John proposed to you?" Shock zigged its way through their bond.

"Sarah, it's not what you think and it happened a long time ago," he said through their link. *"You know I love you."*

"Well not in so many words. I suspected he was waiting for me to finish high school. But he was off at college when I met my Daniel and there was no going back for me. I don't regret a day, either." She wagged her finger. "You know, I believe I have his picture. Hold on."

With Marie out of the room, Sarah pouted at John. *"She broke your heart, didn't she?"*

"I was young. I got over it."

"If that were the case, you would have found someone else. But you never married."

"I was busy being a doctor." But the reality was he'd never married because he couldn't find anyone like Marie. His mother had always told him there was a reason for everything. She certainly couldn't have foreseen him being turned into a vampire at the age of thirty-two, but if not for that life-changing event, he never would have met Sarah. His love for her surpassed anything he'd ever felt for anyone else and he couldn't imagine his life without her in it.

* * * *

Grandma and John? Sarah shook her head. She just couldn't see it.

"Here we go." Grandma entered the room and placed a yearbook on the table. "There's my John."

"Oh my God. Look at yo—him." After placing her drink on a coaster, Sarah moved the book closer and ran her finger over his senior class picture. Eighteen and so young, although he really hadn't changed that much. The photographer had captured John smiling large and Sarah couldn't help but smile back at the picture.

"Spitting image, don't you think?"

John squeezed her hand. He didn't come right out and ask her to change the subject, but it probably wasn't far from his lips. He had no real reason to be nervous but then he'd probably never met anyone from his past, either.

"Does appear the Pennington genes run strong. So where are you?"

"Thank you," John said through their link.

Grandma turned a few more pages. She'd been two classes behind John and her picture was smaller. "That's me."

Sarah favored her father more than her mother, but still expected to see a family resemblance. No such luck. If John had seen any Marie in her, it wasn't evident in the picture. "Ah, look at you. You're beautiful."

"Thank you, but we're all beautiful, honey." Grandma closed the book and stood. "Now, I hope you brought your appetites. Supper's almost ready. Why don't you go wash up?"

"You weren't supposed to go to all that trouble. I said we'd eat out."

"Nonsense. It's no trouble. Not for my only granddaughter. I sure hope I'm around when you two start your own family. I bet you make beautiful babies."

Grandma disappeared into the kitchen and Sarah could only look at her lap. Funny thing was, they would have made beautiful babies. But telling her grandmother the truth would only break her heart. Sarah couldn't do that. Better to go along with it, she supposed.

She showed John to the bathroom where they took turns washing their hands.

John hugged her from behind. "You know, it's possible you were healed when you completed the bond. Babies might very well be a possibility."

"Then why aren't my cycles regular?" She shook her head. "Even if I am, in vitro is awfully expensive."

"We can afford it. I want you happy, Sarah. I want you to have your babies."

"I'm happy with you. And we'll talk about it later. Right now I'm more worried about dinner." Which was the truth. If not for her, he wouldn't have to fake being human.

He chuckled. "I'll be fine."

"I don't want you to fake-eat." Because when vampires ate regular food, it would come back up. Eventually. They couldn't digest it.

"I know you don't, but I'm going to do it, so deal with it. I promise I'll be discreet. Just enjoy your meal. Please. You said I looked pale earlier, but so do you. I still worry you're not eating enough."

"I can't help it when I'm not hungry." The stress her mother caused hadn't helped her appetite any, either. "But I haven't lost any weight, have I?"

"No." He kissed her cheek and nuzzled her temple. "I'll keep that in mind."

A door opened and slammed shut. "Mom! You left the phone off the hook again."

Sarah tensed. No, no, no. This couldn't be happening.

"Your mother?"

She nodded and looked at John's reflection in the mirror. *"Think if we're quiet she won't know we're here?"*

He shook his head. Yeah, she didn't think so, either, but it sure was worth a shot.

"Didja ever think that maybe I didn't want to talk to anyone?" Grandma said. "You need to leave. I'm expecting company."

"Company? Who?"

"That's none of your business."

"It's Sarah, isn't it? She won't see me, but she'll see you."

"I never said anything of the sort."

"It's your fault she's the way she is. Yours and Patrick's. You both coddled her whenever I disciplined her. What is this? You said you were *expecting* company. She's already here?"

"I was drinking the tea."

"With two glasses? And what's this?"

"Put that down and leave. Now."

"My purse! Damn it."

"I can send her away, but if Marie notices…"

"No, don't. It's okay. Shit."

So much for thinking today would be a good day.

* * * *

It pained John to see Sarah apprehensive about confronting her mother. Sure, he could coerce her mother to be loving, but it wouldn't be real and Sarah deserved real.

An older woman with short blonde hair and pale blue eyes who was wearing a T-shirt and capri pants stopped in the doorway. "Sarah? What are you two doing in the bathroom?"

"We were making mad passionate love, what do you think?"

"Don't get snippy with me."

"I can get any way I want." She took John's hand and led him back to the living room. Should he say hi or keep quiet? He chose quiet, but smiled. Sarah picked up her purse. "Grandma, I'm sorry, but we have to go."

"No, you don't. Sit. Carol, out. You've caused enough trouble."

"I've caused trouble! She disowned me; I didn't disown her." Carol leveled her gaze at John. "Are you the one who turned her against me?"

Sarah stood in front of him in a protective manner. "You leave John out of this. He hasn't done anything."

"He's done plenty. He took you away from someone who could've made your life better. This man owns a bar. A bar! What kind of future is that?"

"You're saying you'd rather I stay with a rapist than someone who loves me?"

Marie gasped. "Oh, Sarah. He didn't."

"Steven didn't rape you," Carol said. "He loves you. Wants to have a family with you. You only screamed rape because you couldn't get your way. And now you've ruined his career. I hope that makes you happy."

"Oh my God." Sarah brought her hands to her face. "You still talk to him?"

"We correspond. He has no one else."

Marie glared at her daughter. "What were you thinking? Don't you love Sarah?"

Enough already. This woman didn't deserve to

have Sarah as a daughter and if Sarah got mad for what he was about to do, he'd make it up to her. Forever, if necessary.

He stared at Carol. *You will be disgusted that everyone is against you and leave. You won't talk to your daughter or your mother unless they contact you first*

She stood there glassy-eyed and John prayed Marie wouldn't notice.

Sarah took his hand. *"What are you doing?"*

What he always tried to do. Protecting her.

Carol blinked. "Of course I love Sarah. All I ever wanted was a good life for her. But apparently that makes me the bad guy. I don't need to stay and take this abuse. You can call me when you're ready to apologize."

She slammed the door behind her.

Sarah looked at him with tears in her eyes. *"Thank you."*

"Anything for you." At least she wasn't mad at him. Nothing of the sort flowed through their link, only love and appreciation.

"Hey." Marie wrapped Sarah in a hug. "I'm so sorry, Sarah. So, so sorry. I had no idea." She looked up at John. "Are you going to take care of my girl, here?"

"I am."

"Good." She stepped away and patted Sarah's face. "Wish I could be at the wedding. I've never been to Vegas."

Sarah wiped her eyes. "If you want to go, we can take care of the expenses."

"I wish it were just the money, sweetie. This old body can't handle traveling like it used to. Come on, let's eat before the meal is totally ruined."

Sarah took John's hand as they followed Marie into the kitchen. *"Wow. Grandma didn't even notice anything was wrong with Mom. You're getting better."*

More like determined. *"But you noticed."*

"Only because I knew what to look for. I'm surprised you didn't have her apologize. Is that because I wouldn't believe it?"

"If she ever apologizes, it'll be because she wants to, not because I coerced her. I wouldn't give you false hope. Instead, I gave her a command I expected would be easier for her to follow. Seemed I was right."

"Probably because she was thinking it already. Maybe now she really is out of my life."

Unless Sarah wanted her mother back in it, but by the way things stood, he doubted she'd ever want that. He certainly wouldn't push her anymore.

Chapter 4

After two weeks of life-in-the-dark as usual, John found himself once again dodging the sun's rays in the backseat of his SUV. This time Sarah was driving to the Dayton Airport, where they would fly out for the wedding. *Their* wedding. How was it possible to be ecstatic and panicky at the same time?

He'd never flown before. While that alone would be reason enough to be nervous, the fact the flight was taking place during the day made it worse. And not from fear of burning. After their trip to Cambridge, they'd experimented with the sun. It took ten seconds for the sun to burn his exposed skin. Nine seconds longer than it used to. Even better, covering his skin gave him a few minutes and kept him from losing much-needed energy. But covering up as if it were winter during the hottest time of the year was impractical. He certainly didn't want to draw the attention.

If he could have found a later flight he would have

"Am I going to see you at all before the wedding?" he asked.

"You're seeing me now." She cocked her head and batted her eyelashes. "And we are sharing a room."

"One Lori will probably kick me out of."

"Over my dead body. And we both know that's nearly impossible." She kissed him on the cheek. "Are you sure Perry won't keep you away from me? Isn't he supposed to be taking you out for your bachelor party?"

John groaned. "Don't remind me."

"Hey, I trust you. Just have fun."

"Even if fun includes strippers?"

She frowned. "Okay, then don't have fun."

"Don't worry. I only have eyes for you, sweetie. I wouldn't put it past Lori to take you to a strip club, though."

"Then I promise not to have fun, too."

"Just like you didn't have fun watching *Magic Mike* with Lori?"

"Okay, I might have a little bit of fun." She giggled. "But that's only because I know you're better than anyone else. I still wish you'd dance for me, though."

Ever since she'd seen that flick, she'd been asking. "We'll see."

"Yeah, you keep saying that. I know that means no."

Ahh, but he had to keep her guessing. Sure made life fun. No, she made life fun.

* * * *

John and Sarah boarded the plane and took their seats in the last row. Sarah wasn't sure if John would be able to avoid the sun completely, but once they settled in and he closed the windows in their row and the empty row in front, her fears subsided. They were lucky. The flight wasn't full.

Lori waved when she and Kyle boarded. The meet between Kyle and John had gone well, although Sarah didn't need John to confirm that Kyle wasn't a vampire. His blue eyes didn't have that tell-tale shimmer, something only a Perfect Mate would notice. Another giveaway: the tan he sported. All vampires eventually became pale from lack of sunlight.

But one thing John did confirm for her, Kyle really was smitten with Lori. And all it had taken to get that information was a handshake between the two.

Why couldn't she do neat stuff like that? She'd wanted to be a vampire, too, but because she was a Perfect Mate, the venom wouldn't work on her. It sure would have been cool if she'd ended up with some neat tricks like mind control or super hearing. Then maybe John wouldn't worry about her so much.

Lori meandered toward John and Sarah. "I can't believe you're all the way back here. Why don't you come sit with us? It probably won't be as noisy and I'm sure the flight attendants won't mind."

No, no, no. This was supposed to be their mile-high time. How could she tell Lori that, though?

John saved her the trouble. "They probably have everyone seated where they are to make sure the weight is distributed evenly." He flashed his pearly whites at Lori. Her eyes widened with a glassy look and she grinned like a loon.

She blinked several times. "Yeah, okay. You're right. See you later, then."

As she staggered to her seat beside Kyle, Sarah

shook her head. "I'm glad you got her to go back, but did you have to vamp her to do it?"

He raised an eyebrow. "I *what* her?"

"You know. That thing you do when you want your way. And I'm not talking about control. I'm talking about that smile of yours. You flash that and women fall over themselves to do whatever you ask."

He laughed. "So that's what you call it, huh? You're not jealous, are you?"

"No, of course not." Not in the way he assumed. Just another vampire trait she wouldn't mind owning. "Just doesn't seem fair to the women is all."

"I'll keep that in mind. But just so you know, I'm only interested in how I affect one particular woman." He squeezed her thigh. "And I can't wait until the seatbelt sign is turned off."

And she couldn't either, but once the flight took off, her stomach got queasier by the second. Great. Her first time flying and she got airsick.

John unbuckled his belt. "I'll go in first and then—Sarah? Are you okay?"

"I think I'm going to be sick."

Searching through the pockets in the seatbacks, he found the sickness bag amidst the magazines. He handed it to her. "Can you make it to the bathroom?"

She opened the bag while John unbelted her. He stood to let her out, but before she could stand, her body had other ideas. She bent over and vomited into the bag. "Oh God, I'm sorry."

John rubbed her back as he settled into his seat. "No need to apologize. It's not like you could help it. Can I get you something?"

The flight attendant, wearing a name tag identifying her as Karen, held out a wet cloth. "I'll trade you."

Sarah folded the bag closed and took the cloth. "Thanks. Guess I got a little airsick."

"It happens. Would you care for some ginger ale? That works for some people."

Sarah nodded.

When Karen left to get the drink, Sarah rested her head on John's shoulder. "So much for joining the mile-high club."

John chuckled. "I'm sure there will be other flights."

Not if they made her sick, there wouldn't be. Her stomach still churned. Even John's scent didn't help.

The ginger ale calmed her stomach some, but when they arrived in Dallas to change flights, Sarah nearly passed out when she stood. Luckily, John was too busy getting their carry-on luggage to notice.

The layover didn't give Sarah enough time to grab anything substantial to eat. Not that she wanted any food in her stomach. What if the next flight made her sick, too? Instead, she managed to get some sleep on the flight into Las Vegas.

He woke her to disembark. While it was only eleven at night local time, her body said it was two in the morning. Bed sounded good. So did food, for that matter. If she fainted, she'd never hear the end of it from John. She rose slowly and stretched. No dizziness, but that ginger ale had filled her bladder.

As they walked through the airport, Sarah spotted the ladies' room and excused herself. Lori joined her.

After finishing her business, Sarah stood to pull up her jeans and the walls around her danced. A long blink later, she was sitting on the ground, leaning against the stall, and Lori was pulling on the leg of her jeans.

"Sarah. Sarah, answer me. Are you okay? Shit. Do I need to get John?"

That last part came in loud and clear. "No, I'm okay. Don't get John." Sarah slowly got to her knees before trying to stand again. Thinking about what she might have sat in gave her the chills. At least the floor was dry. After buttoning her jeans, she slid the bolt and opened the door to one worried Lori.

"What happened?"

"I think I fainted."

"What?"

Sarah explained what had happened on the plane as she scrubbed her hands. If she could scrub her jeans, she would have. "Please don't tell John. He'll only worry. This is supposed to be a fun trip."

"You've been feeling sick for a while now, haven't you?"

"What do you mean? It was the flight. I got airsick."

"But you haven't been eating much lately. You buy those big lunches but barely eat half of them."

"Life has been crazy. You know that. Once I'm married, I'm sure my stomach will settle down and I'll eat a huge meal. We'd better get out there before they start to worry."

Too late. John's face was lined in all sorts of concern. How long had they been in there? She should have asked Lori that before they left.

"Sorry, guys," Lori said. "Most of the stalls were being worked on and there was a line for the remaining few."

Relief flashed across John's face. She owed Lori big time.

Chapter 5

Sarah stepped outside the air-conditioned terminal and the heat assaulted her as if she were its long, lost mother. Hundred and four degrees according to her app. She'd expected hot during the day, not the middle of the night.

"Oh my God. It's an oven out here," Lori said, fanning her face as they walked to the taxi/shuttle area. "You would get married in Vegas in the summer. I think I'm melting."

"You didn't have to come." Sarah might have originally wanted to elope, but John had been right. Having friends and family at the wedding would be more fun, and she would have been terribly disappointed if Lori couldn't make it.

"Like I would miss your wedding. Good thing you're not getting married outside, huh?"

John tugged his T-shirt as if he was sweating. "You got that right."

Sarah squelched a laugh. What a faker. Then again,

he had to. He couldn't feel the difference between twenty below zero and one hundred and four above. Being a Perfect Mate hadn't changed her in that regard. Hot and cold still affected her and, like Lori, she was melting. The heat wasn't helping her head any, either. Any sudden movements and she might hit the pavement again. She'd make sure to eat something before turning in for the night.

The lights on the strip mesmerized Sarah as the shuttle transported them from the airport to their hotel. The Mighty Grand was grander than she'd ever imagined—the website didn't do it justice.

While John checked in, Sarah sat on a bench and waited. Even close to midnight the place was rocking with gamblers.

"I wonder if anyone sleeps in this town," Lori said as she sat beside Sarah. "How are you holding up? The heat can't be helping."

"I'm fine. I'll eat something once we get settled in the room, okay?"

Kyle arrived with John and they headed to their rooms, which were across from one another. Sarah bid Lori and Kyle a good night.

The spacious room contained a king-sized bed and a couch. Sarah strolled over to the window and the view of the strip. She'd never seen anything like it. The city was a sea of light. To think, she would be married in this city. In two days she would be Mrs. John Pennington.

John came from behind and wrapped his arms around her. "Perry's texted me about a dozen times. I probably should go see him. You look ready to crash anyway."

"Actually, I'm kind of hungry. Would you please

find me some fruit or yogurt before you meet up with him?"

He kissed her on the cheek. "It would be my pleasure."

John left and she turned back to the window. She could probably stare at the view all night, but that wouldn't get the bags unpacked.

A knock at the door startled her. Had John forgotten his key? When she opened the door, Lori barged in and grabbed Sarah's arm, dragging her toward the bathroom.

"What are you doing?" Sarah asked. "Is there a reason I need to accompany you to the bathroom?"

Lori placed her purse on the counter, pulled out a small bag, and handed it to Sarah. "Here, take it."

"What is it?" Sarah peered inside and confusion set in. "A pregnancy test? You said you and Kyle hadn't done it yet."

"It's not for me, stupid. It's for you."

"For me?" Sarah laughed. "Have you gone nuts?"

"Just humor me, okay? Open the door when you're finished." Lori smiled and stepped out of the bathroom, closing the door behind her.

Pregnant. As if that were even possible. Sarah stared at the box and shook her head. Sometimes Lori came up with the weirdest ideas, but arguing with her wasn't going to shut her up. Taking the test was the only thing that would do that. So Sarah followed the instructions on the box. In three minutes she could show Lori she was nuts.

Sarah opened the door and sat on the toilet seat. "What makes you think I'm pregnant? Because I fainted? I told you I got sick on the flight."

Lori came in, shut the door, and glanced at her

watch. "Yeah, and you've been queasy for a while, too. You have all the symptoms."

"I have the symptoms of someone who's been under stress. You know my equipment doesn't work like it used to. This really is a waste of time."

"What, you have something better to do? Where's John anyway?"

"Getting me something to eat. What about Kyle? I noticed you're sharing a room with him."

Lori grinned and leaned against the counter. "I am. He's waiting for me."

"And you're spending your time here in the bathroom with me when you should be with him. You *are* nuts, you know that?"

Lori shrugged before she looked at her watch again. "Time's up." She held out the stick. "You want to do the honors or me?"

"Give it here." Sarah snatched it out of her friend's hand. She'd show her how silly this whole business was. "See? It has a plus sign. Wait. What?" She grabbed the box off the counter. Plus sign equaled pregnant. "How can that be?"

Lori took it out of her hands. "Whoo-hoo! I knew it! You're pregnant!"

The bathroom door sprang open and John stood there, eyes wide, looking dumbfounded. Sarah shot to her feet and managed to mutter "John?" before her world darkened.

* * * *

John zoomed and caught Sarah before her head hit the tile. He couldn't have heard Lori correctly, except a pregnancy test kit sat on the counter. What the hell was going on? After scooping Sarah up, he carried her to the bed and laid her upon it.

"Damn, you have quick reflexes," Lori said. "I don't think I've ever seen anyone move that fast."

If the bathroom had been any larger, or if Lori's attention had been only on him, he might have had to wipe her memory. Instead, he let her remark go.

"You should probably know she fainted at the airport, too."

"What? Why didn't she tell me?"

"Because she thought it was due to the flight and didn't want you to worry. At least now we know why, huh? Can you believe it? And her doctor said she couldn't get pregnant."

Most likely the doctor had said she *shouldn't* get pregnant, not that she couldn't. Except there was no way he could have gotten her pregnant. Not as a vampire. The only person who could have was Steven, when he'd raped her nearly five months ago, before she completed the bond. Even if she had conceived then, wouldn't she have lost the baby after Danielle stabbed her? Or had the bonding healed that, too? Still, at five months she should be showing and she wasn't. "I need to get her to a doctor."

"She's not sick, John. She's pregnant."

He pinched the bridge of his nose. "So you said. But nothing's adding up. She shouldn't be pregnant."

"Not all contraceptives are perfect. Doesn't mean one of your swimmers couldn't, you know."

"Right." Except he had no swimmers. Which left Steven. Would she want to carry his baby? John wouldn't care whose baby she carried—as long as it didn't endanger her life. He'd love it because it was Sarah's.

Sarah stirred. Her eyes fluttered opened and she looked around.

John sat on the bed beside her. "It's okay, sweetie. You fainted. How do you feel?"

"A little light-headed. Nothing different than I've been feeling all day." She sat up and smiled.

"I'll leave you two alone," Lori said as she headed for the door. "See you in the morning, okay?"

"Thanks, Lori." Once her friend left, Sarah took John's hand. "Do you think it's possible?"

"I think we need to get you to a doctor." He reached over to the nightstand and pulled out a phone book.

She took the book from his hands. "Not here. When we go home. I'll call my—"

"No. You can't see your regular doctor."

"Well, I don't want to go to an emergency room, either. It's possible the test gave a false positive. It happens, right? Let's wait and see a doctor tomorrow."

"I don't know if I can trust a cab in the daylight and I don't want you going alone."

"Then we'll rent a car big enough for you to hide in. Please. Right now I just want to eat and sleep. That's why I fainted."

Maybe he was overreacting a bit. She hadn't eaten anything since getting sick, so it was possible she'd be light-headed from lack of food. "You're really hungry? Not just saying that?"

She smiled. "Have I ever lied about being hungry?"

He shook his head. If anything she would have lied about not being hungry.

"I had you get the food earlier, didn't I? I feel fine. And hungry. Honest."

"Okay. We'll wait until the morning."

Maybe the test would prove to be a false positive, but he couldn't count on that. He'd worry until the doctor told him not to. Now, if he could only get the night to move along quicker.

* * * *

Sarah sat on the examination table and swung her foot, thankful she'd been able to get an appointment with a local OB/GYN, and a female one at that. Sure beat going to the emergency room. Forget about the lack of privacy, nothing good ever happened there. Here she sat in a room with pictures of babies, not a walled-off curtain in sight. Made for a more relaxing visit. Wouldn't know it by looking at John, though. He'd done nothing but pace.

"You keep that up, they'll charge us for new tile."

Again she met with silence. The fact the test result had come back positive hadn't changed his attitude any. No hugs. No kisses. Just a request for an ultrasound. "It might be ectopic," he'd said. And while that word gave Sarah the chills, her gut told her that wasn't the case. But John needed proof, so she'd wait until he got it. Maybe then she'd get his hugs and kisses.

She hadn't gotten them when she awoke this morning. And man, if that hadn't stung. So what if her stomach bothered her? His scent still had the ability to calm it. He had better not act that way during her whole pregnancy. She'd go mad!

Hopefully he was still baffled at how he could get her pregnant and only needed the proof laid out for him to relax. To think they had the Perfect Mate bond to thank for this miracle. Unless…

Unless she was pregnant with Steven's baby.

Her doctor had always told her that while she

could technically conceive, it would be difficult and not something to attempt because she wouldn't be able to carry to term. But when she'd completed the bond—a mere eleven days after Steven had raped her—had John's blood fixed whatever had kept her from carrying to term?

Except she'd been stabbed. Would that matter? Probably not. It had happened after the bonding. She'd healed from the knife wound, so it was very possible that if she was pregnant at the time...

Oh God. That's why John was antsy. He didn't want Steven's baby.

What little she'd eaten for breakfast churned in her stomach.

Before she could broach the subject with John, Dr. Messner wheeled in an ultrasound machine. "Let's see what we've got in there, shall we?"

The paper crinkled as Sarah lay on the table. Dr. Messner squirted the wand with jelly then rubbed it over Sarah's exposed belly. John came over and took Sarah's hand.

"John?" she asked through their link.

"How are you feeling?" he asked aloud and kissed her on the forehead.

All right, so no internal talking. "Okay."

Except she wasn't okay. Not even close.

"There's your baby." The doctor pointed at the screen. She didn't seem all that concerned. That was good news, right?

However, the screen showed static and squiggly lines. Sarah squinted, but it didn't help clear it any. "Where? I don't see anything."

"That little peanut."

Oh. It was so tiny. "John, do you—" Sarah turned

around, but he'd left her side and resumed his pacing. She looked back at the doctor. "Can you tell what the sex is?"

Dr. Messner chuckled. "Not yet. Give it another eight or nine weeks."

What? When Lori's sister had been pregnant, she'd found out after eighteen weeks. Then again, she'd been showing. Sarah's stomach was still flat. "How far along am I?"

John answered, "Seven or eight weeks."

Eight weeks? That meant the baby wasn't Steven's. That meant the baby was John's. She was having John's baby! And apparently he knew this, too.

The doctor smiled. "That's right. But you don't have to worry. Everything looks normal. The baby is where it's supposed to be. Congratulations." She handed Sarah some towels. "Go ahead and get cleaned up. I'll be back in a bit."

With happy tears ready to spill any second, Sarah hopped off the table and wiped the goop from her stomach. "I can't believe this. I thought tomorrow would be the best day of my life, but this? I think this tops everything."

He continued pacing as if he hadn't heard her. Except his hearing was perfect, so he was just ignoring her.

She placed the dirty towels on the examination table with a heavy heart. Why did her pregnancies bring out the worst in her husbands, or in this case, future husband? "Why aren't you happy? I thought you wanted children, too."

John stopped and stared at her stomach. "How are you pregnant?"

"What do you mean? You don't think—" She

couldn't even bring herself to say it.

His eyes widened and he shook his head. "No. God, no, Sarah. I don't think you cheated on me. But this is clearly not Steven's baby, so how are you pregnant? I don't have sperm."

"That you know of."

"What?"

"Your blood changed me. Why wouldn't my bonded blood change you? You said it was different after. That it's stronger."

"It is." His brow was furrowed as he began pacing again. A moment later his mouth dropped open and he collapsed onto the small chair. "Oh shit. This can't be happening."

"What part can't be happening? That you now produce sperm or the fact I'm pregnant?"

He leaned his head back. "Ahh, Sarah. I was more than willing to love this child if it were Steven's. But now..."

"But now what?"

"Don't you see? If I'm the father—"

"If?" What did she have to do to convince him otherwise?

"I'm sorry. That didn't come out right. But with me as the father, this baby can't be...normal."

"The doctor said everything looked normal."

"The placement, yeah. But she didn't check its DNA. This baby is half vampire. I can't even imagine what it'll do to you."

"You want me to get rid of it?" *Oh God. Don't let it be like Steven all over again.*

"Not if it's normal. But what if that baby starts sucking all your blood—"

"John, be reasonable. The bond wouldn't work

like that."

"We don't know that. We don't know anything."

"Ah, but we do." When he raised his eyebrows at that, she knelt in front of him. She had to get him to see reason. "The Perfect Mate story is a love story, not a horror story. That tells me nothing bad will happen. And I've survived a stabbing. I can't believe this pregnancy will do me in or I wouldn't have gotten pregnant. We've been given a gift, John. I believe our bond will keep me out of danger. You have to believe that, too."

He cupped her face and rubbed her cheeks with his thumbs. "I want to believe that. I do. But—"

"But you won't feel better until you have your baby in your arms, huh?"

"Well, I wouldn't go that far. Maybe after your second trimester."

She would have laughed if she thought he was joking. With a reassuring squeeze on his thighs, she rose. "We need to tell Barnet."

"Barnet?" He shot to his feet. "No, no. We tell Victoria."

Sarah had to admit that that was a better plan. Victoria could rein in Barnet better than anyone. "Okay. Probably best we tell the other Perfect Mate couples first. I mean, if I could conceive…"

His eyes widened. "But the females are vampires. Their bodies don't work like that."

"That you know of. You used to be sterile, but you're not any more."

He walked over to the ultrasound machine and stared at the image. "You know he's going to want to test and observe."

"And how is that any different than you'll be?"

Because if she knew her man, he would be testing and observing every chance he got.

"Am I really that bad?" He looked over his shoulder and she smirked at him. "Okay, you made your point. But can we keep this quiet until after the wedding?"

"You trying to protect my reputation?" she teased. "Or your own?"

She'd finally put a smile on his face. "You wanted a fun wedding. If Barnet finds out beforehand, he'll be all business. You know that. So can we at least enjoy our wedding before telling Victoria?"

She jumped into his arms. "On one condition. You kiss me and hug me and tell me you can't wait to be a father."

"That's more than one."

"So sue me."

"Nah. How about I kiss you and hug you and tell you I'll do my damnedest not to freak out over your pregnancy?" When he planted his mouth over hers and held her tight, unease niggled its way through their bond.

At least he was trying. She got the hug and kiss. Guess it *would* take holding his baby to get him to stop worrying.

Maybe.

Chapter 6

John sat in the dark holding the ultrasound picture while Sarah slept in the bed. He'd snuck out earlier and found a store that sold a microscope so he could conduct his own test. Turned out he produced very active swimmers, as Lori would say.

Why he'd needed that test to prove to him what Sarah's tests should have, he didn't know. Guess she wasn't too far off when she claimed he'd be doing his own testing and observing. As his father used to jokingly say, he just needed to cross all his Is and dot all his Ts. A joke John had been sure would never be passed down since his brothers had died childless and he had become a vampire rendering him sterile. Except now he wasn't sterile.

"Guess I'll be able to pass that joke on now, Dad." A tightness settled in his chest as he ran his finger over the image. A father. Through the miracle of bonding with a Perfect Mate, he was going to be a father. And his baby would be…

Half vampire.

Would it have fangs or no fangs? Live on blood or regular food? Grow to a certain age for eternity or grow old and die like every other mortal? He bent over and rubbed his hand over his face. Oh why couldn't he let it go and be happy? He wouldn't dare broach these questions to Sarah, but the Committee would certainly wonder the same thing.

His cell phone vibrated.

Another text from Perry. *If you don't come downstairs now, I'm coming up to get you. I don't care if I wake Sarah.*

Shit. After texting Perry to hold his horses, John stood, shoved the phone in his pocket, and stared at the photo. What should he do with it? He wanted to enjoy his upcoming wedding before telling anyone. That included Perry—Mister Loose Lips if ever there was one. John found Sarah's toiletry bag and shoved the picture inside, just in case.

He gave Sarah a kiss on the cheek and departed. If he was going to have a bachelor party, might as well have fun. Hell, the party was more for Perry anyway. After Danielle's execution, Perry had made himself scarce because he thought he didn't deserve John's friendship. John didn't know how else to prove it except to ask Perry to be his best man. Hadn't even occurred to him that Perry would want to hold a bachelor party. Maybe if it had, he would have made a stipulation. As if that would have stopped Perry.

The elevator doors opened to one grinning Perry. He spread his arms wide. "Johnny! About damn time. Now we can start the party."

"Are you sure this is necessary?"

"Sure it's necessary. It's a rite of passage." Perry grabbed his arm and headed for the exit. "Besides, once I get a little booze in you—"

"What?" John pulled free and stopped. Having fun at a party was one thing, but booze meant feeding from an inebriated mortal. He hadn't fed from anyone other than Sarah since she'd completed the bond. And the last time he'd gotten drunk, he'd nearly outed the entire vampire race.

"Relax. I promise not to let you get out of control. Just loose enough to keep you from being a stick in the mud. And I also promise you won't be near any women. At least not any closer than the end of the stage." Perry laughed. "I'm sure Sarah will be okay with that."

Stick in the mud? Is that what he'd become? Okay, so maybe he could stand to be a little looser. "Where are we going?"

"To Count Dracula's Club."

"No way. You're kidding, right?"

"Why would I kid about a thing like that? It's owned by one of our members, too. Cool, huh? Now let's go."

The place wasn't located on the strip, but on one of the side roads away from the heavy foot traffic. Still, for being out of the way, the club was a popular place; a steady stream of people entered. Maybe it had something to do with the brightly lit neon sign that sported a set of blood-dripping fangs. Before John could join the crowd, Perry grabbed his arm and dragged him to the back.

"Is this the secret vampire entrance? Why aren't we going in the front?"

"Secret vampire entrance," Perry said, laughing. "That's a good one. But if we go in the front, Barnet will nab you before I get you ready."

Like he had to be prepared to attend his own bachelor party. Oh wait. He did.

Perry opened the back door and ushered John inside. Expecting to smell fried foods and beer, John nearly gagged from the stench of urine and vomit emanating from the restrooms.

"They really should get someone to clean up back here," John said over the boom-boom-boom of the bass as it reverberated off the walls.

"Yeah, I'll be sure to tell someone." Perry opened the men's room and shoved John inside. "Get in that stall and wait. Don't lock it. I'll send a guy in and you take over, okay?"

Perry couldn't possibly expect him to feed in this mess. "Are you sure this is—"

"You don't need to breathe, so shut up and get in there. I told you I'd be the best best man ever. You'll thank me later. Honest."

"We'll see," John muttered, gingerly stepping his way to the stall. Drunks couldn't aim to save their lives. He'd never leave his restrooms looking this messy, mainly because of his sensitive nose. If a vampire owned this bar, he must not be on site. Or breathing.

At least the stall Perry chose was somewhat clean. A few moments later the door opened and a man stepped inside.

"He's all yours," Perry said.

The man blinked at John, his cue to take control. He didn't have to feed from the guy, except he was a little bit hungry. He hadn't fed from Sarah since they'd left Dayton and wasn't sure if he should now, not with her pregnancy. Guess some boozy blood wouldn't be so bad. After determining the donor wasn't on any erectile dysfunction drug, or taking any illegal substances, and his alcohol intake was light—two beers—John bit the man's neck. His blood wasn't near as tasty or potent as Sarah's, but it was doing the job. A nice buzz settled over John and loosened him up.

Seemed Perry was right. John wouldn't admit it, though.

He took his fill and licked the site clean. The holes miraculously disappeared, thanks to his healing saliva. After mentally instructing the man to take care of his business, John left the stall and disconnected their link.

Perry was leaning against one of the sinks with his arms crossed. "Feel good?"

"Yeah, I do." John walked to the cleanest sink and washed his hands.

"That's my Johnny." Perry headed for the door.

"What about you?"

"I'll find me a nice little woman; don't you worry."

John quickly dried his hands and followed Perry down the short hallway to the main club where rock music blared from the speakers. The place resembled a bad Halloween getup. Fake Draculas stood in the corners. Bats with red-lined capes hung from the ceiling. Everything was decorated in black and red. Even a few of the couples dancing on the floor were dressed to match the surroundings.

"Is this for real?" John asked.

"Cool, huh? If we slip up and say something we shouldn't, no one here will notice. Or care. Everyone plays the vampire game here."

John looked downright normal in his jeans and white buttoned-down shirt. And Perry, well, someone might wonder if he'd just come from the golf course. Ever since he'd discovered that he couldn't hide the imperfections of his wardrobe from a Perfect Mate, he'd disposed of the ripped Hawaiian shirt and cargo pants and replaced them with polo shirts and pressed khakis.

Barnet and the male vampire he sat with also stood out from the decorations—Barnet in a blue buttoned-down shirt and dark slacks and the other guy in a black long-sleeved T-shirt and jeans. Was that how vampires would eventually be discovered? They would be the ones dressed normally in a vampire bar?

"Johnny, that there is Sammy. He usually bartends here, but he's off tonight. Sammy, this is Johnny. He owns a bar." Perry chuckled. "You two should really get along."

Eyes as dark as his hair, the vampire shook his head. "Actually, my name is Sam. Sam Kincaid. So you're the famous John Pennington."

"Famous?" Shit. That couldn't be good.

"You have to admit," Barnet said. "You're not only the first vampire to be turned illegally, you're also the first male vampire who found a Perfect Mate."

"Lucky me. So what's the plan tonight, Perry?"

"Well, first I need to get me a drink and I think I just spotted her. Excuse me while I go get acquainted. I won't be long."

As soon as Perry planted his butt on the bar stool next to a blonde, Barnet leaned over. "We don't know what Perry has in mind, but Sam and I were thinking about taking this party over to his place. Maybe watch a movie?"

"I could go for that," John said. Sure beat a strip

club. The only woman he wanted to see stripping was Sarah. "You live in the city?"

Sam nodded. "For a couple of years, yeah. You live in Dayton, right? You're not by any chance looking for a bartender, are you?"

"As a matter of fact, I am, but my bar isn't as popular. I probably can't pay as much, either."

"Pay isn't an issue. It's the quiet I'm looking for. I can't stand it here anymore."

"You finally thinking about settling down?" Barnet asked.

"You would like that, wouldn't you, old man? I swear, Barnet here won't be happy until every vampire is married."

"Well, I wouldn't go so far as to say that, but why not? What's wrong with living in eternity with someone?"

"Nothing, I guess. But it's got to be the right someone, otherwise you'd have settled down yourself, right?"

"Touché," Barnet said.

Over at the bar, Perry was nuzzling the blonde's neck when she gripped his shoulders and closed her eyes.

John pointed at the scene. "Is he…doing what I think he's doing? In public?"

Sam turned around. "Relax. People playact that here all the time. No one's going to think he's any different. It is kind of funny he picked her."

"Why? What's wrong with her?"

"She's a he. I can't believe he didn't notice."

Barnet squinted in Perry's direction, as if that would help his eyesight. "Are you sure?"

"Sure I'm sure. He comes in here all the time.

Man, I wish I had a camera. Perry could stand to use a little ribbing."

Maybe so. Perry had certainly played his share of pranks. Still, it sat wrong on John's conscience. But before he could get up and warn his friend, Perry finished. He kissed the woman/man goodbye and got groped in the groin, which led Sam to snicker. Perry sauntered over to the table, grinning like a goon.

"Good kisser?" Sam asked.

"I'll say. If it weren't for this little party, I'd have me a date tonight. But nothing's more important than my friend Johnny." Perry sat in the open chair and, as always, tipped back on the rear legs. "Now, this is what I have planned—" Before he could finish, the legs slipped out from under him. With arms pinwheeling, he crashed to the floor.

"Graceful," Sam said, clapping. "What time is the next show?"

Perry leapt to his feet and picked up the chair. "Go ahead and laugh. I don't see you with a potential date."

Sam put his palms together and looked at John and Barnet. "Let me tell him. Please?"

"Tell me what?"

"You fed from a dude."

"No I didn't."

"Yes, you did."

Perry plopped down on his seat. "But she—she grabbed my crotch."

"Because *he* likes dudes."

"But, but…" Perry looked to John, and he could only grimace his regret. Perry's eyes widened and he looked down at the sizeable bulge in his crotch. Must have been a *really* good kisser. He held up his index finger. "Hold on." He then staggered to the drag queen.

"I guess he didn't believe me," Sam said.

A minute later Perry stumbled back in shock, shaking his head. "I can't believe this. Why didn't anyone warn me?"

"Why, because you were turned on by a guy?" Sam asked, grinning.

"That's not the point."

"Are you sure? You seem turned on to me."

Perry collapsed onto his seat. "That's just it. If I had known, I would have, I mean—she—he took Viagra."

Viagra? Oh shit. Perry's bulge took on a whole new meaning.

"Oh my God." Sam bent over laughing. "You're so screwed."

"Why would he take that? He's young!"

Sam shrugged. "They think they can get a better erection with it. *You* are, aren't you?"

"Very funny." Perry adjusted his crotch and moaned. "Damn it, I feel like I'm going to explode in my pants. If I had me a Perfect Mate, this wouldn't have happened. What am I gonna do? Are there any single females in the area?" When Sam shook his head, Perry's eyes widened. "Then get me a mortal. Lori's here, right?"

"Lori's here with her boyfriend," John said.

"Perry, stop it," Barnet said. "I'll not have you put someone in danger. You'll have to take care of yourself manually."

"But—but—"

Barnet held out his palm, silencing Perry, and stood. "Sorry to cut this party short, but I better take him back to our room before he makes a scene. I'll see you tomorrow at the wedding. Come on, lover boy."

Perry slowly rose to his feet and let out a moan. "Oh shit. I think I just came."

"The first of many, I'm sure." Barnet grabbed Perry's elbow. "You can clean up in the restroom."

"I'll be as good as new tomorrow, Johnny. I promise. I won't let you down."

"Good luck." John waited until they left and then turned toward a grinning Sam. "I guess I might as well go, too."

Sam's grin disappeared. "Before you go, can I ask you a few questions? About Perfect Mates?"

So, the questions were already starting, huh? How often would he have to put up with that? "Sure, go ahead."

"How did you know Sarah was one? Did you try to feed from her and found you couldn't wipe her memory?"

"No, nothing like that." Wouldn't that have been embarrassing. "We were on a date and it wasn't going well, so I thought I'd read her mind to see what I was doing wrong."

"And found you couldn't, right?"

"Right." John smiled. Sam made it sound so calm. Technical. When in fact there'd been nothing calm or technical with that discovery. Inside, he'd turned into a blubbery mess, but Sam didn't need to know that. "After our date, I broke it off and tried to stay away. As you can tell, that didn't work out."

"What about Perry? Did he meet her before you two bonded?"

"Yeah. Her scent affected him, but not to the

extent I was affected. I think."

"You think?"

"I never pushed the issue with him, because I really don't want to know. Once I had unknowingly started the bond, she affected him less, but I became more paranoid and protective of her. It helped that Sarah disliked him. Heck, she probably still does, but she hides it well."

"So Sarah was attracted to you, but not to Perry? That must have been a blow to his ego."

John nodded. "It was, but who knows what she would have felt if she had met him first. He might not have come across as an ass."

"I don't know. Can he control that?" Sam burst out laughing and John could only do the same.

"Are you like Perry now? Hoping to find your own Perfect Mate?"

Sam leaned back in his chair and smiled. "Actually, I'm pretty sure I already met one."

Chapter 7

When the Committee announced the existence of Perfect Mates and which vampires had mated, John had braced for the onslaught of questions. He expected many vampires would act like Perry—determined to find their own. Or maybe a few crazy ones might get it in their heads to take Sarah from him. What he hadn't expected was an admission of having met one.

"How come you're telling me and not Barnet?"

"I don't know." Sam scrubbed his head. "Because you're safe?"

"Barnet's safe."

"I respect Barnet, but he's still an unmated vampire."

And that would be a major issue with male vampires. No matter how the Committee spun it, Barnet was competition, same as the other two male members: Abraham and Jack. And it wouldn't matter that Jack was married. His wife was a vampire, not a

Perfect Mate.

"If it makes you feel better, I had planned on talking to Victoria. But then you showed up here and I thought, why not? Hell, I'm not even sure I found one. If you promise not to tell Perry, I'll tell you my story. If you believe I found one, then I'll talk to Victoria."

Not tell Perry? "I can't make that promise. He's my friend. I'm sorry."

John stood to leave, but Sam grabbed his arm. "No, I'm sorry. You're right and I shouldn't have asked. So maybe I just won't give you all the details?"

It was enough for John to agree. He returned to his seat. "You think it's safe to talk here?"

"Probably the safest. Our kind don't normally come here."

"I can't imagine why."

Sam laughed. "It is pretty gaudy, isn't it? Another reason I want to leave this place. I need some normal."

"If you found a Perfect Mate, I doubt you'll ever get normal."

"Yeah, but that kind of abnormal I could live with. I hope."

John couldn't argue with that. He certainly loved his abnormal life. "So what's your story?"

"About four years ago—"

"I'm sorry," John interrupted. "You've been tracking her for four years?"

"No. I have no idea where she is. I swear, until the announcement, I really had no idea she might even be one. Anyway, I was walking to one of my feeding spots, a nice little service station in the middle of nothing, when headlights appeared. A woman drove up to fill her tank, so I walked inside the store and waited. I could have fed off the old man running the store, and had several times, but why would I when there was a lady around?"

"You're starting to sound like Perry."

"Well, I hate to admit it now, but I was more like him then. Never even occurred to me that my actions might get me in trouble."

"Because of this woman?"

Sam nodded. "When she came inside to pay, I got a better look at her. God, she was pretty. Real pretty. She wore jeans and a tank top that hugged her curves just so; I practically salivated. Her blonde hair was pulled into a ponytail and when she glanced at me, those blue eyes of hers seared my very being. But the kicker? Got a whiff of peaches and cream. About did me in."

"You like peaches and cream?"

"Love the smell. Reminds me of home. Why? Is that what Sarah smells like to you?"

"No, she smells like strawberries to me. But she smelled like jasmine to Perry and wild meadows to Barnet."

"Wait. She didn't smell the same to all of you?"

"No. And I'd bet your girl, if she is one, would smell like jasmine to Perry and wild meadows to Barnet. We figure one of the traits of a Perfect Mate is a scent that reminds a vampire of home."

Sam leaned back and ran a hand through his hair. "Which means they'd recognize her for what she is right away."

"That would be my guess, if she is a Perfect Mate."

"Well, that changes things."

"How so?"

"Perry and Barnet will know right away if they run into a Perfect Mate. If they found out about mine—"

"Except you don't know if she is one. She could have had a brain injury or tumor." John didn't believe that for a second, though.

Sam rested his arms on the table. "I thought the same thing. But what about her scent?"

"Perfume? I'm not saying it's likely, just a possibility. Why don't you just tell me what happened next."

"She'd asked to use the facilities, which were located outside. I thought it was a gift from Heaven that I wouldn't have to coerce the old man to forget seeing me go inside the ladies' room—they're kind of fragile when they're old—and I followed her to the back. It was nice and dark and the moon was nonexistent. Either the security light burned out or it never existed, I don't know. I only know I took it as another gift. I saw the light seep through the cracks in the restroom and knew when she came out, she'd be practically blind. I wasn't wrong, either.

"Now, I'm not proud of what I did next, but she had such a draw, I couldn't help myself."

A Perfect Mate's draw was some powerful stuff, and Sam's description sounded much too familiar. John leaned forward. "You didn't…take advantage of her, did you?"

Sam's eyes widened. "I didn't rape her, if that's what you're asking. When I'm with a woman, it's because she wants to be with me. But I did want to kiss her. Get a taste of her peaches and cream. When she came out of the restroom practically blind, I situated myself so she would walk into me. Bam! She did just that. I laid the allure on thick and kissed her. I felt a heat so intense, it traveled through my body and her scent intensified. She was like a magnet and I was the metal drawn to her. Then she kissed me back. Hungry-like. Everything I wanted. Feeling like I had her under control, because she was doing everything I wanted, I bit into her neck and tasted the sweetest blood ever. It was like a dream. Then she screamed, brought me to my senses. I was afraid I'd lost control, except—"

"You never had control."

"Exactly. I tried to pull out gently and heal her, but she yanked away and grabbed her neck. Before I could think straight, she slapped my face. No one had ever done that to me before. Well, no mortal. I grabbed her hand, felt that heat again, and tried to read her, to find out what was wrong, and it was like hitting a brick wall. I got nothing. Afraid she was going to yell vampire, I improvised."

"Improvised?"

Sam chuckled. "Yeah. I told her I'd mistaken her for someone else and apologized. She told me I was a pervert and started to storm off. I couldn't let her walk away, so I picked her up. I don't know what the hell I was thinking, I just reacted. I carried her back to her car and then put her down, but not before licking her neck. I had to heal her, but wanted another taste, too. You know? She slapped me again, got in her car, and drove off. The loss I felt shocked me. No one had ever affected me like that before. I almost ran after her, but how would I be able to explain that? I couldn't wipe her memory. I considered myself lucky she only thought I was a pervert, because it could have been a whole lot worse. But now I wonder. What do you think?"

"From what you describe, I'd say you found a Perfect Mate."

Sam shot to his feet. "Hot damn! I knew it."

"Easy." John grabbed Sam's elbow and pulled him back to his seat. "You don't know she's yours."

"How could she not be mine? She's all I think about. That scent. That taste."

"That's you. What she remembers is an assault. Then there's the possibility another vampire has already claimed her."

Sam shook his head. "If she'd been claimed, she would have been brought forward for protection after the announcement was made. And Perry hasn't whined about anything like that. Which means I gotta find her fast, but how? All I know is what her name, credit card, and license plate were four years ago. Is that enough to go on?"

"It could be. Victoria has the resources—"

"No! After what you said about her scent, I don't want the Committee involved yet."

John couldn't blame Sam for feeling possessive. Wasn't he also keeping information from the Committee, albeit temporarily? "You're safe going to Victoria. She'll understand your concern. Don't you want to find this woman?"

"Sure I do, but how do I know the Committee won't get involved? She's part of them! Then they'll hold me while they send some vampire to go find her. And then that vampire ends up bonding with her. Can't let that happen. She's mine."

John laughed. Was this how he'd sounded to Barnet?

"What's so funny?" Sam asked.

"You. Your paranoia. Oh, I know where you're

coming from. I've been there." Still was, actually. "None of that will happen if you tell Victoria. She won't let it. I won't let it."

Sam drummed his fingers on the table. "Can I think about it?"

"Sure, I'll give you a couple of days. But also think about this. You tell Victoria; I'll keep your secret. I'll even help you find her." John grimaced a little inside. Perry might kill him for that, but then it would be Perfect Mate business, and Perry wasn't involved in that. Not until he found his own.

"And if I don't?"

"Then I suggest you hide out and find this woman on your own before your next meeting, because I will tell Victoria. She'll decide whether or not the rest of the Committee needs to know."

"Man, you drive a hard bargain. You mean it, though? You'd help me find her?"

"You tell Victoria; we'll both help you."

"Okay, okay. Let's call her before I chicken out."

John took out his cell phone. "You're doing the right thing. And I hope you find her soon. But if you find out she's married with a family, don't go after her. I'm all for you finding your mate, but not at the expense of breaking up a marriage."

Sam sat back, defeated. "You think that's possible?"

"Why wouldn't it be possible? People marry for all sorts of reasons." John dialed Victoria's number and held the phone out. No need to put it on the speaker. They'd be able to hear her fine and it would eliminate a chance of anyone eavesdropping.

"How about if she's *happily* married I'll drop it? But if she's still free, or miserable, I'm not letting her go again."

John hoped Sam could drop it. The allure of a Perfect Mate was hard to resist, no matter what the circumstances.

Chapter 8

Barry Manilow's singing voice jolted Sarah awake. She snuggled into the covers. Why was she listening to "Copacabana"?

"John?"

No answer. That would explain the music. He'd set the alarm. She certainly hadn't done it. Heck, she hadn't set an alarm since moving in with John. So where was he? She searched the nightstand and the empty side of the bed. No note.

As much as she would love to stay in bed, she had a wedding to prepare for and it started with a shower. Leaving the radio on, Sarah slowly crawled out of bed and stood. Thank God the room didn't tip over—eating smaller meals more frequently seemed to have done the trick—but her stomach still churned like it had every morning for the past few weeks. At least now she knew why.

She rubbed her belly. "Hey, little peanut. You could at least be nice to me since I'm the source of your food and I'm giving you a home. Plus, I'm your mother."

Mother. Used to be that word gave her the willies. Hopefully the word grandmother wouldn't do the same to her child. That was if she even bothered telling her mom. Better to decide that on another day. Say, like in a decade or so.

She sang along with Barry and cha-cha'd her way to the bathroom. Taped on the mirror was a note from John. What a sweetie. He'd gone down to get her breakfast. Hopefully something cold and light. Her stomach couldn't take anything warm and heavy. She turned on the shower, stripped, and stepped into the warm water.

Ten minutes later, she finished alone—much to her dismay—and dried off. With the towel wrapped around her, she went back into the room and found John sitting on the couch. "Why didn't you come and join me?"

He smiled. "As tempting as that was, you haven't been feeling well, and I don't need the wrath of Lori coming down on me. It's bad enough I'm seeing you at all. I only stayed to see how you're feeling and to let you know I told Victoria. After she freaked out over the news, she agreed that Barnet can wait until after the wedding."

"I'm glad you told her. What made you change your mind?"

"I just realized she had a right to know sooner rather than later. And I know she won't lock you up. So, how are you feeling?"

Sarah shook her head. John and his crazy theories. Although he knew Barnet better than she did, so maybe he had reason to worry. "I'm fine. Just the morning sickness. No more dizziness.”

Relief washed over John’s face and he stood. “Good. I’ll let you eat in peace, then. I brought you some fruit and yogurt.”

“No. Don’t go.” She pulled him back down and snuggled next to him. His scent not only calmed her stomach, but made her hungry, and not for food.

“Since when did you want me to stick around while you eat?”

“Since now.” She buried her nose into his neck and inhaled deeply. God, he smelled good. “Please stay. I’m just glad Lori didn’t kidnap you so you wouldn’t see me before the wedding.”

He grimaced. “She tried. Apparently my promise of no hanky-panky wasn’t enough and I might have laid the charm on a bit thick.”

“What do you mean? You vamped her?”

He shrugged. “More like nudged. Don’t be mad. She was driving me nuts.”

Lori must have been, for John to resort to mental persuasion. He despised doing that. “I hate to break it to you, but she won’t give up that easily. She takes her maid of honor duties seriously.”

“Tell me about it. Anyway, go on and get dressed.” He dislodged her from his body. “Your breakfast is waiting.”

She didn’t want to get dressed. His scent still called to her, and he hadn’t even hugged or kissed her yet. What was up with that? Couldn’t have been from his promise to Lori. Could it? Well, she would have none of that.

She unhooked the towel, letting it fall open, and ran a hand down her neck. “What about you?”

“I’m good.” He stood and walked over to the

desk, keeping his back toward her.

His rejection stung. "How is it you're good? You haven't fed since we left Dayton."

"I fed last night. At the party. For the booze. But I do wonder if I should take any more of your blood."

Was this what she had to expect for the next seven months? Because she wouldn't put it past him to think taking her blood would somehow harm her or the baby. "John, you've never taken enough to hurt me."

"That was before you became pregnant with a baby who could very well demand all your blood. I don't want to make it worse."

Again with his wild theories. "John—"

"I know, I know, the bond won't let anything bad happen." He paced in front of the desk, still not looking at her. "But you haven't been feeling well. You can't deny that."

She rewrapped the towel around her and sighed. "It's just morning sickness. A normal reaction to being pregnant. I feel better after I feed you, though."

He stopped and narrowed his eyes at her. "You do?"

She nodded. It wasn't a lie. She did feel better. Just not for long. Almost like her body became disappointed that the blood she tasted—via their link—wasn't actually being consumed. But if she asked to sample him, he'd think she was nuts. "Please don't shun me. I don't think I could stand not being held by you until I gave birth."

He sat beside her and wrapped her in a hug. "Ah, Sarah. I'm sorry it seems that way. I don't know how else to keep my promise to Lori. You're too damn hard to resist."

She let out a huge sigh. Figured that Lori had caused his rejection. "So, no kissing before the wedding?"

"Definitely no kissing. Or feeding. I promised to behave. It's the least I can do after I…you know."

"Fine. No feeding you until after the wedding. But you can feed me, right?"

He grabbed the bag from the coffee table and handed it to her. The yogurt could wait, but he'd brought a banana. Ooh, she could have fun with this. The heck with Lori. What she and John did before their wedding was between them, not Lori. Sarah took out the fruit and peeled it.

"I used to like bananas," he said.

"Yeah?" Maybe she could get him to enjoy the fruit again, in a different, erotic way. She took his hand and squeezed while slowly inserting the banana into her mouth. If this didn't get a reaction, she might as well let Lori win.

And he did react. Just not in the way she expected.

His eyes widened. "I can taste that," he said. "Chew it."

Damn, she could hit herself. If she could taste his blood when he fed from her, why couldn't he taste the food she ate? She chewed, swallowed, and waited.

"Tastes just like I remember. Take another bite." The smile on his face brought joy to her heart. Eating in front of him would no longer be an issue. He could enjoy the food right along with her. And if he didn't want to taste it, he could easily break their link.

After she finished the banana, she snuggled close to him. Her life was perfect now.

"As much as I love you in or out of a towel, I wish you'd get dressed. Remember, I promised Lori no hanky-panky."

Sarah laughed. "So? You promised her. I didn't. You can plead you'd been taken advantage of." She buried her nose against his neck and licked his skin. "Mmmm…"

He palmed the back of her head but instead of pulling her away, he held her in place. "God, Sarah, that feels good. You're not playing fair."

"No. Lori's not playing fair." That urge came over her again. Would her teeth be sharp enough to bite him? Before she could find out, her cell phone rang.

John grabbed her shoulders and gently pushed her away. He kissed her on the forehead and retrieved her phone from the coffee table. "It's Lori. She must have some kind of sex radar."

So close. So damn close to sampling his blood. Sarah snatched the ringing cell phone in a huff. If it were anyone else, she would have let it go to voice mail.

"Is John with you?"

"Yes. This is his room, too."

"It's your wedding day. It's bad luck for the groom to see the bride beforehand." Apparently John's little suggestion had only lasted long enough for his escape.

"Stop it, Lori. There is no bad luck today." Except for the no-sex-before-the-wedding part. Or the sampling-of-his-blood part, either. Sarah gritted her teeth. *Damn her!*

"Tell Lori I'm leaving," John said as he stood. "That should please her."

"Hold on a minute, Lori." She covered the phone. "You don't have to leave on her account."

"Ahh, but I do. I feel bad about what I did to her. Besides, I have arrangements to make and I'm sure

Lori wants to help you get ready."

"I don't need that much time to get ready. We're still wearing jeans, right?"

John laughed. "Yes, I'll be wearing jeans, but I'll also be wearing a sport coat and a nice shirt." He raised one eyebrow. "If that's okay with you."

"Sure it's okay. I hope I don't look dumpy next to you, though."

"Not possible." He leaned over and kissed the top of her head.

She uncovered the phone. "John's leaving. When should I expect you?"

"I'm on my way. And if you're not dressed, don't bother. I have your outfit with me." With that, she hung up, leaving Sarah to stare at the phone.

Outfit? What outfit? She frowned. It was her wedding, not Lori's. Didn't she have any say in what she wore?

John opened the door to Lori, whose arm was up and ready to knock. John's trick used to impress Sarah, until she discovered his ears and nose worked better than any human's. Probably better than any animal.

"Hey, John," Lori said as she passed him to enter the room, carrying a large shopping bag. When she got a look at Sarah sitting on the couch with just a towel on, she narrowed her eyes at him. "Did you behave?"

"Yes, he behaved," Sarah said. "But don't expect a thank you card."

"And that's my cue to leave. I'll see you two ladies this afternoon. Bye, sweetie." He blew Sarah a kiss. Before he left, he whispered something to Lori and she nodded back at him.

"What did he say to you?" Sarah asked after the door closed.

Lori gave her the once-over, examining every inch of her. "You look better today."

"Food and sleep will do that. So what did he say?"

"He asked that I feed you before the wedding. He probably doesn't want you fainting at the altar. Can't say I blame him."

"Very funny. What's in the bag?"

Lori placed the bag on the coffee table and sat on the couch. "Your wedding outfit."

There was that word again and it put Sarah on edge. "I told you I was wearing—"

"Yeah, yeah, I know. You're wearing jeans. But..." Lori raised her index finger in the air. "You didn't specify what kind or the top. So I hope you don't mind that I bought you this." She reached into the bag and pulled out the most beautiful top Sarah had ever seen.

Delicate lace covered satiny ivory material at the tips of the long, flared sleeves and hem. Side-by-side grommets—strung together with ivory ribbon in a zig-zag fashion—lined from the top of the shoulders down the length of the sleeves. The same pattern occurred along the sides of the garment from under the arms down to the hem. Two large, antiqued, pewter-coin buttons adorned the front, just below the low-cut neckline.

"I also got you a jean skirt and espadrille wedges to go with it. It's casual, but...not."

The flared skirt reached Sarah's calf and went beautifully with the top, as did the shoes. But she couldn't resist playing with her friend. "I don't think my cat socks will go with this. How about the penguins?"

Lori rolled her eyes. "You're not supposed to wear socks."

Sarah giggled and hugged her friend. "I'm just kidding. This is perfect. Thank you."

"You're welcome." Lori stood. "So hurry up and get dressed. We have to be at the hairdresser's in less than thirty minutes." She lifted some of Sarah's hair off her shoulder and examined it. "Did you wash your hair this morning?"

"No."

"Of course you didn't. Don't bother putting this top on yet. You can change into it after your hair is washed and dried." She shook her head. "What would you do without me?"

"Get married in jeans and a T-shirt with my hair in a ponytail?" Sarah grinned. Her way would have been simpler, but Lori's was probably better. John would be happy she spent some effort at preparing herself.

* * * *

John leaned against the counter waiting on the concierge. He'd been told he could get his jacket pressed and ready by morning, but something must have happened. No sign of the jacket or the person responsible for getting the work done.

So far the day had been one mini disaster after another. After he'd fixed the botched flower order—how hard was it to get roses?—and found another photographer who hadn't come down with the flu, he'd run into Lori, who demanded he stay away from Sarah. Like that was gonna happen. If anything, he wanted to be with her more. To make sure she wasn't lying about feeling well. Because that would be like her—to hide it from him.

But this morning Sarah had seemed all right. The color had returned to her cheeks. Eating smaller meals more frequently must have done the trick. And damn, if he'd discovered he could taste food through her earlier, she may never have skipped meals to begin with. Still, it didn't mean he wanted to take her blood while she was pregnant, but he'd save that argument for after the ceremony.

The concierge returned from the back office he'd disappeared into earlier. "I'm sorry, sir, but it appears your sport coat has been…damaged."

Of course it had. "Damaged? How?"

"I'm afraid our employee met with an accident. While he came out unscathed, your coat hasn't." He handed over two pieces of material. The coat had been split down the back. "I am terribly sorry."

"Great. I was supposed to get married in this." Not that Sarah would mind. She hadn't been expecting a coat at all. Still…

The concierge held out a piece of paper. "I understand. Please accept this coupon for a replacement at our store."

John stared at the coupon as the concierge left to help another customer. At least the store was located inside the building. But what kind of luck would he have in finding something that fit on such short notice?

"Hey, Johnny." Perry patted John on the back. "What the hell is that?"

John tossed the ruined garment in the trash. "Nothing. I see you survived the night."

Perry shrugged. "What's to survive? So I had sex with my hand." When John raised an eyebrow, Perry rolled his eyes. "Okay, so I had a lot of sex with my hand and maybe it was a little painful. Would a woman have helped? Most definitely, but Barnet was right. I'd have only hurt her. And that wasn't happening. So what can your best man help you with this morning?"

"Can you help me find a replacement coat? Mine got damaged."

"That was yours?" Perry looked at the coupon. "Sweet. That blazer you had was beyond boring."

John looked at his friend. He wouldn't have. Would he? "You didn't have anything to do with mine being damaged, did you?"

Perry's eyes widened. "Now, would I do a thing like that? I'm your best man."

Yeah, but he was also Perry. John shook his head. "I don't have time for this. I'm sure there won't be anything in there that won't need to be tailored."

"Nonsense. Let's go."

As they headed for the menswear shop, they passed a children's store. John stopped at the window display. Little cowboy boots. Little hats. Little everything. He wanted to buy them all.

"I don't think they have your size," Perry said.

John chuckled. "You ever regret not being able to sire a child?"

"Who said I didn't?"

"You had children?"

Perry shrugged. "I wasn't exactly celibate as a mortal. And protection wasn't available like it is now. It's quite possible I got at least one woman pregnant. Probably a dozen. Never could stay away from those chamber maids."

"Doesn't that bother you, not knowing? You could have fed from a descendant."

"It didn't bother me until now." Perry scrunched his face and shuddered. "Thanks for that. Now let's go get your coat before you really gross me out."

When they arrived at the menswear shop, John headed toward the suit coats, but Perry steered him toward the leather jackets.

Perry held up a dark brown one. "This is anything but boring and something Sarah would approve. You should definitely get married in it."

John had to admit, it did look nice. He looked at the price tag. "Holy crap! This is worth more than ten of my coat."

"But you have that coupon." Perry pointed. "Besides, I don't think there's anything here as cheap as your blazer, or as casual."

Everything was kind of ritzy. It didn't seem fair to trade his coat in for something so extravagant. John shook his head. "I can't. Besides, it probably doesn't even fit."

To prove him wrong, Perry helped him put it on. Damn thing was soft and fit perfectly.

"You think this will go with Sarah's jeans theme?"

"Are you kidding? Wear a white T-shirt with that and it'll be perfect. You can thank me later," Perry said, smiling. "Now, wonder if they have one in my size. A best man should look their best. Right?" He found one in a lighter shade of brown on the rack and slipped it on. "Ohhh, sweet, isn't it? We'll be the envy of every gambler here."

"But yours won't be free."

"Don't you worry." He took both jackets and the coupon and headed for the register.

Don't worry? If Perry thought he could get away with coercing someone into letting him take that jacket without paying, he was clearly delusional. But he didn't coerce anyone. He handed over a credit card.

John stepped up to the counter and signed his coupon. "When did you get that?"

"A few months ago. Abe set it up for me." Perry took both hangers and handed over John's jacket.

John waited until they exited the store before asking, "You have money?"

"I know. Cool, huh?"

"Where'd you get it?"

"From the Committee. Seems I've been on their payroll every time I did some errands. Who knew? They didn't trust me to not squander it, so they've been investing my paycheck."

"How'd you find out about it?"

"When I asked to borrow money for my new clothes. I didn't want to steal them. What if a Perfect Mate caught me in the act? I'm on the straight and narrow. Everything legal. It's quite exhilarating."

"Wow. I'm impressed. I hope you find her soon." And before Sam found his. John could only hope that Perry never learned of his involvement.

"Yeah. And then you could be my best man."

Best man? Ah, crap. What kind of best man kept a secret concerning a potential Perfect Mate? The next time someone wished to confide in him, he'd run away as fast as he could.

"What's next, Mr. Bridegroom?"

"I need to take this back up to my room. After that, maybe we could get something to eat." That drunk last night hadn't filled him like Sarah's blood did. He also had to take care of Sarah's surprise, but he could do that without Perry. "Are you up to some company or already full? Because if you're full—"

"What's wrong with Sarah?"

Oh crap. And he'd been worried about saying something while under the influence of alcohol. "I…uh… Well, you see, Lori doesn't want me to see her before the wedding."

"Man, and I thought I lied bad. What's going on?"

"So you did ruin my coat."

"Quit changing the subject. Why aren't you feeding from Sarah?"

John nearly laughed. If anyone was the master at changing the subject, it was Perry. But as much as John would love to confide in Perry about Sarah's pregnancy, now was not the time. "She hasn't been feeling well. So are you hungry or—"

"Wait a minute. She can still get sick?"

"She's not sick. It's stress. Her mother isn't too happy with us getting married."

"Already have mother-in-law issues, huh? Sorry, man. You'd think a Perfect Mate would come with a set of perfect in-laws. At least you know she won't be around forever."

And wasn't that the truth. Hopefully the same couldn't be said about his child.

* * * *

Sarah had never been pampered at a salon. In the past, she'd go to have her hair washed and cut with one hairdresser doing the work. Having multiple people showering attention her way made her uncomfortable at first, but eventually she gave up and enjoyed the show. She even let Lori take over how she should look. It really wasn't worth the fight.

After the facial, hair styling, manicure, and pedicure—why Lori deemed she needed pretty feet was beyond Sarah—Lori dragged her to the food court. Sarah was famished, having only eaten the banana, but the scent of fried food caused her stomach to churn once again. If this kept up, she would end up puking at her own wedding.

Lori must have seen the look on her face because she grabbed Sarah's hand and led them away from the food court to a small deli. The scent of freshly baked bread filled the air and calmed her stomach. A puke-free wedding was looking like a possibility.

After placing their orders, they sat at one of the small round tables available and waited for their food. With all the hustle and bustle at the salon, Sarah hadn't had a chance to talk to Lori.

"What's Kyle doing?"

"Gambling. I never heard so much relief in a guy when I told him he was on his own until the ceremony."

"And last night?"

Lori smiled as if remembering a pleasant memory. "Last night was great. I really think he might be the one. Oh, I'm not saying I'd marry him. Yet. But if it turns out he can stand to be around me and he loves babies, I'd be stupid to give that up. Besides, he's the hottest guy I know."

"You used to say that about John. And Perry."

"Nothing against those two, but Kyle is way hotter. Especially when he looks at me. Turns me into goo every time."

Sarah was truly happy for her friend. Lori deserved to have someone in her life. "And you're stuck spending the day with me. I bet you can't wait until the wedding is over, huh?"

The cashier called their number and Lori stood.

"Just because you're some kind of sex maniac when it comes to John, doesn't mean I am with Kyle. I can wait until tonight. Honestly, I can't believe the two of you. Without me around, you and John would probably be at it like bunnies."

Sex maniac? Hardly. Sarah considered herself a sex junkie, at least where John was concerned. Big difference. Right?

Lori returned with the tray of food. As Sarah reached for her soup and sandwich, she said, "You just wait until your wedding day and see if you can stay away from your future husband. And if you can, then you can judge me all you want. But I'm not going to apologize for loving him. Today is about a slip of paper."

"You make it sound so…clerical. Is that how you see this? Shouldn't it be a pledge of your love for one another?"

"I don't need the ceremony to know that John loves me. And he knows how I feel. But I will try and make this day special. Not just for John, but because it is the first day I'll be known as Sarah Pennington."

Lori raised her sandwich in a toast. "To the future Sarah Pennington. Hmmm… That does have a nice sound to it. But then, so does Mother."

Never had for Sarah, but then she'd had the worst role model. Maybe it would sound better if John wasn't so nervous about the whole pregnancy.

"Have you told anyone yet?" Lori asked.

"No, and I'd appreciate it if you'd keep it a secret."

"Why? You said everything was okay."

"John wants to enjoy the wedding and would prefer we announce it later." Like, maybe never. Honestly, the man worried too much.

"Guess he wants you to look all proper, huh? Okay. Mum's the word." Lori giggled. "Get it? Mum?"

"You crack me up," Sarah said sarcastically. Shaking her head, she picked up her sandwich. Just how much of Perry had rubbed off on her friend?

"Well, there's my girl."

She nearly dropped her sandwich and her heart skipped a beat. Was it possible? Had he changed his mind? She turned in her seat and slowly stood. Familiar green eyes gazed at her. "Dad? What are you doing here?"

"I heard my daughter was getting married. Isn't it proper her father walk her down the aisle?"

She rushed into his arms. "But you said—"

"Forget what I said. Your fiancé convinced me I should come. He's right. It's where I belong." He hugged her tight, like he had when she was younger. Now her wedding would be perfect. Unless…

"What about Mom?"

"She thinks I'm at a boring convention, so she won't be spoiling your day. And if she finds out I didn't go…" He shrugged. "Oh well."

Sarah wiped her eyes. She took her father's hand and led him to the chair next to hers before sitting in her own. "I don't want you getting in trouble."

"Sarah, baby, don't you worry about that. I should have stood up to her long ago. And maybe I finally will. But first I'll see you married and happy and out of harm's way."

Did it make her a horrible daughter that she wished her parents would get divorced? Then she could visit her father more often. At least he was here now. That John would do this for her meant more than anything. God, she loved that man.

Chapter 9

The groom's room was no bigger than a small bedroom, but it suited John's needs just fine. He sat back on the leather couch and would have enjoyed the quiet if not for the racket on the other side of the room. Perry inspected every drawer and cabinet door in the credenza, which supported a high-def television on top.

"What are you looking for?" John asked.

Perry closed the last door and plopped down on the couch. "I thought they'd have some games. Why else have the TV?"

"Bored already, are you?"

"Nothing wrong with passing the time, is there?"

"What about your phone? I assume you have at least a dozen games on it."

"I can get games on that thing?" Perry pulled out his cell and pushed the button. When the screen didn't light up, he shook it. "Hmmm… You don't happen to have a charger, do you?"

John chuckled. "Not on me, no."

"That figures. Why didn't anyone tell me I could get games on this before?"

The door opened and Debra, the wedding coordinator, entered the room. "You all set?"

John was more than set. They followed the woman to the side door of the chapel where John expected a nearly empty room. Instead, he was greeted with the groom's side filled with men.

"Is this the right chapel?" John asked, but shouldn't have bothered. Kyle sat alone on the bride's side and Barnet and Sam sat on the groom's. Then he got a better look at the rest of the audience. They weren't just men. They were vampires. Nearly two dozen of them. He turned toward Perry and raised his eyebrows.

Debra looked in her book. "Yep. Pennington wedding. Is there a problem?"

"So I told a few people," Perry said. "Face it. You're big news."

"Big news?" Debra stared as if she should recognize him.

John smiled. "He's joking. Will you excuse us a moment?" He pulled Perry over to the door, out of sight of the audience, and stared at his supposed friend. "Why? Why?"

"Chill. They aren't a threat. You know that, right?"

He knew no such thing. "How can you be sure?"

"Don't tell me you're still paranoid. Johnny, only two of us got a whiff of Sarah before you two completed the bond. If anyone is a threat, it'd be Barnet and me. Are you worried about us?"

"No, of course not. But—"

"But nothing. Those guys are only here because

Perfect Mates are big news. Your bonding is big news. That's it. Get used to it." Perry spun John around and nudged him toward the altar. "Now go get married."

John looked over his shoulder at his best friend. "When did you become so sensible?"

"Hey, I told you I'd be the best best man ever."

That he had, and John was thankful for the common sense Perry had drilled into his head.

The officiant held out his hand. "Mr. Pennington? I'm David Ryan. I'll be performing the ceremony today."

John took the extended hand and smiled. Mr. Ryan exuded calm and confidence, relaxing John in the process. He introduced Perry.

At the main entrance, Lori burst into the room with her normal flourish and paused when the vampires turned her way. Many stared. Probably because she was a beautiful woman. Or it could have been her bright yellow blouse. It made her jean skirt look practically black. Smiling large, she sashayed her way down the aisle and stopped at the altar.

"You sneaky devil. You really made her day." Lori grinned.

He brushed his hand against her arm and smiled at Lori's memory. Sarah had been surprised and very happy with his gift. "I'm glad."

"I didn't know you had so many friends, though."

"I don't. I have Perry to thank for that."

Lori took her place at the altar and wiggled her fingers at his best man. "Hi, Perry."

"Hey, sweetness. Looking stunning as usual."

"Thanks." She tapped John on his arm and whispered, "I got Sarah to eat, so no fainting during the ceremony."

John smiled and nodded. He would have preferred she'd kept quiet about that because Perry didn't need any more fuel to light his curiosity.

"Sarah fainted?" Perry asked.

"Only because she wasn't eating. She's fine, now. Stress, remember?"

"Stress… Right…"

Pachelbel's Canon in D began playing over the speakers. Everyone rose and stared at the door.

John straightened and adjusted his jacket. Maybe on their fiftieth wedding anniversary, they could have a fancier ceremony. Him in a tux and her in a beautiful white gown. She'd go for that, wouldn't she? He'd love to see her dressed up. But for now he'd do casual. Hell, he'd do anything for her.

The door opened and he smiled.

* * * *

Sarah dabbed at her eyes. Lori would kill her if she ruined her makeup again. She still couldn't believe what John had done. But here he was, her father, getting ready to walk her down the aisle.

"I'm so happy you could make it."

Dad kissed her cheek. "So you've said about a dozen times. I'm glad I could be here. You ready to go?"

Sarah took her father's elbow and stepped into the chapel. The scent of roses filled the air, while the real things—grouped in red, yellow, pink, and white— were displayed in vases sitting on tables along the side walls. Lovely, simply lovely. Had to have been John's idea. Kyle sat alone on her side of the room, while the other side—the groom's side—was filled with shiny-eyed men. Vampires at their wedding. Of course there were.

After the Committee announced that Perfect Mates were real, she'd figured vampires would be curious. Just not how much. Guess she'd have to get used to being an anomaly.

"I didn't know John had so many single friends," Dad said.

"I think they're more like friends of the best man." At least she hoped they were. She couldn't imagine John inviting them.

Before she could fret anymore about the significance of their appearance, John captured her attention and she couldn't look away. His iridescent eyes were filled with love and desire. Thank God her father guided her way. She would have run into John's arms or skipped down the aisle. The joy inside her threatened to bubble out of control.

After kissing her cheek, Dad took a seat beside Kyle. Sarah practically bounced beside John. "Been waiting long?"

"Just my whole life," he said.

Her heart filled with so much love, it nearly hurt. God, he knew how to say the right things. She dabbed at her eyes again. "If you ruin my makeup, Lori's gonna get you."

He took her hands and squeezed them gently. "You're beautiful."

"And you're sweet." She took a glance at the groom's side of the chapel while doing her best to keep smiling. *Should I be concerned?*

"Uhh…no. Perry—"

"Say no more. I understand." She took a moment to admire his leather jacket. It screamed casual and fun and was perfect. Now, if she could only get him to

relax and smile. It wasn't so much the vampires that made him nervous, but people in general. One of the reasons she had wanted to keep their ceremony small.

The music ended and Mr. Ryan raised his arms in welcome. "Ladies and gentleman, we are gathered here today to celebrate the marriage of Sarah and John."

Even though she and John were magically bonded, this ceremony made it more real. The officiant's words made it more real. Why had she ever thought this was only about a slip of paper? Thank God John had more sense than her.

"I've been told that the couple have written their own vows. John?"

He took a deep breath but never broke eye contact with her. "Sarah, while today celebrates the beginning of our married life, my life became complete from the moment I met you, and I thank God every day that you decided to take a chance on me. We may have our bumps along the way, but know that I will love you through them all. I will be by your side no matter what happens. I will love you forever."

Sarah blinked back tears. "John, you are my rock. My compass. My friend. My lover. My mate. I never knew what real love was until I met you. Today starts a new chapter in our lives and I can't wait to savor every minute of it. I promise to love and cherish you, to be by your side no matter what. I will love you forever."

John took the gold ring from Perry and slipped it on Sarah's finger. "This ring, which has no beginning or end, symbolizes the bond we share, and the love and trust between us. I place it on your finger as a visible sign of our promises."

Sarah took the matching ring from Lori, slipped it on John's finger, and repeated the same vow. He was hers now, in every way possible.

The officiant raised his hands. "By the power vested in me, in the state of Nevada, I now pronounce you husband and wife. You may now kiss your bride."

John took her smiling face into his hands. "I love you, Mrs. Pennington."

He kissed the smile right off her to the sounds of applause. Man, if they didn't have an audience, she'd start the honeymoon right there. Lori's "whoop-whoop" put a stop to the scorching kiss.

"Guess I'll have to continue it later, when we're alone," he said through their link.

"Can't wait." And then she'd make sure he didn't stop with a kiss.

Mendelssohn's "Wedding March" played over the speakers. Maybe it was a bit much, but she'd married an old-fashioned guy and he'd picked that song. He took her arm and walked her up the aisle. Every vampire had their sights on them. Some nodded as she and John passed.

Perry took Lori's arm and followed them up the aisle. Lori giggled.

John stopped and turned around. "Perry, no."

Perry, no, what? Was he being inappropriate again?

"Sarah's pregnant?" Perry said.

"Ahh crap," John muttered.

And to think she was worried about being an anomaly, when she should have been worried about her friend's big mouth. "Lori, how could you?"

"I'm sorry," Lori said. "I don't know why I said that."

John shook his head. *"Not her fault. It's mine. Perry suspected I was keeping something from him."*

It wasn't John's fault, either. Sarah glared at the offender. Ooh, when she got Perry alone she was so knocking him into the next century. He had no right to dig into Lori's mind.

Barnet approached John with raised eyebrows. Sarah's father wasn't too far behind. The rest of the crowd seemed calm, but did that mean anything?

John raised his arms and laughed. "Okay, guess the cat got out of the bag before we could make an official statement. We were hoping to enjoy today first. But yes, Sarah is pregnant. If you want to know more, you're welcome to join us at the reception, but we have some pictures to attend to first. We'll meet you at the pub after."

Pictures? Now she noticed the lady photographer, who had most likely been snapping away during the ceremony. Her husband, the planner. She'd never even thought about pictures.

Sarah squeezed John's hand as the procession left the chapel. She didn't care that everyone knew she was pregnant—that would eventually become obvious. Making John happy was more important, and he wasn't anywhere near that. As much as she would love to whisk him away and spend the rest of the day alone with him, that wasn't going to happen.

Damn Perry for getting John upset. She needed to make him smile again.

She caressed the soft leather of his sleeve. "I love your jacket. When did you get it?"

John looked down as if he'd just now noticed it. "Today." He continued through their link, *'I'm so sorry. I made the mistake of telling Perry you weren't feeling well. I should have known he couldn't let it drop."*

"It's okay. We knew we'd have to tell everyone eventually."

"Yeah, but not in front of an audience of vampires."

"True. But if you'd rather not mention you're the father, I'd understand."

"Well, I wouldn't. I wouldn't do that to you or to our child. And I'm sorry I had my doubts earlier. You didn't deserve that. So I'm not going to lie. But if Barnet tries to take you to Atlanta, he'll have a fight on his hands, so be prepared."

"You think he would?" John didn't need to answer her. Of course Barnet would. He was crazy-obsessed with Perfect Mates. Damn Perry. She should have known he'd find a way to ruin their day.

* * * *

Pictures went better than John expected. Having Sarah by his side helped in that regard. Plus, being out in public, John couldn't exactly berate Perry. Better to have that confrontation in private. Or outside near an open field. That way when he punched the guy, he could go flying without damaging property.

Punching would have to wait though, since they had a reception to attend. Lori and Kyle had left a few moments earlier, leaving John and Sarah alone with Perry. John would love nothing more than to whisk his wife up to their room and start their honeymoon, but he couldn't put off the inevitable.

"I don't know why you were keeping it a secret," Perry said, as they headed for the pub. "A baby is great news, isn't it?"

Sarah leaned around John and sneered at Perry. "You wouldn't have even known if you didn't go snooping in Lori's head. How could you?"

"If you had told me, I wouldn't have had to snoop."

"Since when is it any of your business?"

John raised his arm between them. "Okay, you two. It is what it is."

"I'm sorry," she said through their link. *"I promise you a good time this evening."* She looked ahead and squeezed his hand. *"Or maybe not. Should I be concerned?"*

Four male vampires, dressed in jeans and buttoned-down shirts, loitered at the entrance to the pub. Curious or dangerous? Perry had said curious, but with John's lack of experience around other vampires, seeing them together like that unnerved him just a bit. Oh sure, he'd gone to his annual meetings. Didn't mean he'd socialized.

"Hey, guys!" Perry said and, pointing from left to right, he continued, "That's Mac, Rick, Aaron, and Danny. They're the four I told about the wedding."

"You only told four people?" Sarah asked. "Then who were those others?"

"That would be our fault," Mac said. "Thought it would be fun to see a Perfect Mate—or would that be Perfect Couple?—get married, so we spread the word. But we aren't here to make trouble. It wasn't until you, John, arrived for the wedding that I wondered if our appearance might be misconstrued."

Barnet and Sam appeared at the entrance to the pub, but stayed behind the foursome.

Rick glanced over his shoulder. "We're just curious, honest. We decided a smaller group would be best to convince you that we're not a threat."

"And you four won?" John said.

Aaron laughed. "Told you he would say that. But really, we have no designs on your lovely wife. None of us do. Frankly, she's no different to us than any other woman." He smiled at Sarah. "No offense, but we wouldn't know you were a Perfect Mate if we weren't told."

"Yeah," Danny said. "Kind of a bummer, if you ask me. Still, we think it's cool you found one. Gives us hope we'll find someone. But we are wondering… Did *you* get her pregnant?"

John lowered his head. He should have known it would come to this. Tell the truth and get shipped to Atlanta for who knew how long or lie and deny his child's parentage? No matter what, he just couldn't do the latter. He straightened, ready to face…whatever. "It appears our bond made that possible, yes."

Barnet's eyes widened. "What?"

"Holy shit," Perry said. "I just thought she'd had in vitro."

"I can see this is news to Barnet, too," Mac said. "Making this Committee business now, huh? We'll leave you to that, then. Again, we meant no harm attending your wedding. I wish you many happy centuries together."

The four vampires, in turn, kissed Sarah's free hand. John wasn't about to let her go, even if they seemed friendly enough.

Barnet blocked their exit. "Before you leave, tell me, does knowing you can have a family with a Perfect Mate make you determined to find your own at any cost?"

Mac shoved his hands into his pants pockets. "I'm still trying to understand the presence of Perfect Mates, no less having a family with one. No offense, but I'm thinking there is more to this Perfect Mate business than just finding one. Certainly if there were enough to go around, we'd have found them long ago."

"I thought so, too," Aaron said. "Which makes me wonder if they're being hidden."

"Hidden how?" Barnet said. "We're questioning everyone at the meetings."

"Sure, of the ones that you know are alive. What about the ones you think have perished? Isn't it possible they faked their death because they found a Perfect Mate? They'd have no way of knowing it was safe to bring them in now."

Barnet covered his face and groaned.

"Thanks, Aaron," Perry said. "You just made his head explode."

Mac laughed. "Let me ease your head, then. No, I won't go looking for one at any cost, but I can't guarantee what I will or won't do if I find one."

The other three agreed with Mac. Barnet nodded. "Fair enough. Thank you." Once they left, he turned his sights on John. "I need to talk to you. Alone."

John nodded. Talking he could do. But would Barnet like what he had to say?

Chapter 10

Convincing Sarah that it would be okay to go to the reception without him wasn't as easy as John had thought. Seemed protecting him was just as important to her as protecting her was to him. Weren't they a pair?

It took Barnet's promise that John wasn't in trouble for her to finally go inside the pub.

"I'm sorry to pull you from your reception." Barnet led John to an area away from traffic and pointed to a couch along the wall where no one could approach from behind. "I thought it best we talk in private."

Private didn't sound good. John sat and propped his right foot on his left knee. "If I'm not in trouble, then why the secrecy?"

"Because I didn't want to insult your wife to her face." Barnet sat on John's left. "Whose baby is she carrying?"

"You think I would lie to those men?"

"I think you would love this baby to be yours."

"It is mine."

"How can you be sure?"

Maybe it was a good thing Sarah wasn't around to hear this, because this was the kind of scrutiny he'd expected and he didn't need her subjected to it. "Number one, she wouldn't cheat on me. Number two, she wasn't artificially inseminated."

"But she was raped. Isn't it possible—"

"That was more than five months ago. She's barely two months along."

Barnet stood and paced. They'd been speaking quietly, but now he whispered, "But I don't understand how that can be. You don't generate sperm."

"You mean I didn't used to. I knew you'd have your doubts. Hell, I had my own, so I tested my semen. Seems it now contains sperm. Lots of them."

"Lots? Damn." Barnet plopped back onto the couch and glanced around, but no one was in sight. "Another trait that makes those Perfect Mates even more…perfect. How come you didn't tell me?"

"Because I wanted to enjoy my honeymoon before the inquisition and possible lockup occurred."

Barnet pinched the bridge of his nose. "You're beginning to sound like Victoria."

"You have to admit, you've been a little obsessed. And the fact I could be responsible for creating a freak of nature? Can't blame you there." John hoped to God that wasn't the case, but who knew? Certainly not them.

"We're all a freak of nature. And I doubt Sarah would be able to carry a baby if it wasn't human."

"Except, she's not really human anymore, is she?"

He bent forward and placed his elbows on his knees, trying to loosen the tightening around his chest. "I'm worried, Barnet. I can't lose her."

"Listen. I truly doubt Sarah is in any danger. That would go against everything a Perfect Mate stands for."

"You sound like Sarah. She thinks this is all normal."

"And it may very well be for Perfect Mates. Now, I don't mean to sound controlling, and I have no intention of locking you up or forcing you to stay in Atlanta, but we must document this pregnancy. There's still so much to learn. If you can get Sarah pregnant, what does this mean for Victoria and Katarina? Which reminds me, I need to tell them first, and soon."

"I understand." John was tempted to tell him not to bother, that he'd already told Victoria, but then Barnet would know they were discussing traits of bonding without the Committee's knowledge. The three of them had agreed to share anything new among themselves before sharing with Barnet, one of the reasons John had Sam talk to her first. "Are you going to send out another announcement?"

"I might not need to. It's why I need to talk to them pronto. You'd be surprised at how quickly word spreads among our people; if you hadn't been holed up as a hermit all those years, you'd know what happened today isn't unusual. And that was for your wedding. A baby, now that's big news. The biggest. I'm guessing what's said in Vegas isn't staying in Vegas for very long."

John laughed. Wow. Had Barnet just cracked a joke?

"Are you going to be able to handle the pregnancy and birth as well as document everything?"

"You think I'd let anyone else do it? But if complications occur, I'll need the proper documentation stating I was licensed to practice."

"I'll get on that right away. You might also need to examine Victoria and Katarina. If they've changed—"

"Then there's nothing you can do about it," John finished. "But if *they* want me to examine them, I can. Do you understand?"

"Duly noted. I'm glad we have someone with your skill we can count on."

John looked up to the lights. "I really thought I'd lost that life. Kind of nice to know it's not totally gone."

"If more Perfect Mates are found and bonded, we might have a population boom to worry about. You might end up being more popular than you ever wanted."

Ahh, but what a problem to have. Provided they weren't giving birth to monsters.

* * * *

Sarah washed her hands in the restroom after another false alarm. This morning sickness, or actually all-day sickness, was really starting to get on her nerves. That, or her anxiety toward whatever Barnet had to say to John was the cause. Not exactly the fun wedding she'd hoped for.

Although, there was still the wedding night. Provided Barnet didn't whisk them off to Atlanta. Somehow she didn't think John would go for that. At least not right away.

She grabbed some paper towels and dried her hands. Time to get back to the party, not that it was much of one. Lori was definitely having fun dancing with Kyle. Everyone else just kind of sat around. Didn't help that the groom was missing. He certainly would have cured her queasy stomach.

Damn Perry and his curiosity.

The door swung open and Lori burst her way inside. "Bad news."

"What?" Sarah said as she flung the towels into the trash. "Is Perry telling everyone you're pregnant, too?"

"Ummm… No. It's your mother. She and your father are kind of fighting. Thought I should warn you. You know, in case you wanted to make a run for it."

"What the hell is she doing here?"

"I think she followed your dad. She's none too happy, either. So, what do you want to do? Face her or run for it?"

Ah, what a friend. If it weren't for what little family Sarah loved, she'd have John put a rush on declaring them dead. But since she wasn't ready to say goodbye… "Guess I'll go save Dad. Keep him busy, okay?"

"Do you need me to get John?"

"No. I can take care of her." Should have done it ages ago. John might have been quicker—heck, he had in the past—but she couldn't rely on him all the time. Plus she just needed to finally end things, if only for herself. Mind control wouldn't do that.

After taking several deep breaths, Sarah exited the restroom and entered a war zone. Her mom was shooting words and her dad was ducking and covering. She'd like to think he was trying not to make a scene when he was most likely afraid of what

Mom would do if he fought back. Mom never played nice.

Sarah stormed over to her mother and grabbed her arm.

"I'm sorry, Sarah," Dad said as he rose from his chair.

The fact he felt the need to apologize only spurred Sarah on. "Not your fault. Come on, Mom. We need to talk."

"Oh, now you want to talk to me? Where's that fiancé of yours anyway?"

"This doesn't concern him." Sarah dragged her mother out of the pub and away from the direction John and Barnet had gone. A small alcove in the corner met her needs just right. She practically hurled her mother toward the bench.

Standing tall, Mom rubbed her arm. "You don't have to be so rough."

"How in the hell did you find me?"

"Watch your language. There's no need for you to be crude."

Sarah gritted her teeth. Instinctively, she'd almost apologized, and she was through with apologizing to this woman. "Just tell me how you found me."

"It didn't take much. I knew something was up with your father's unexpected convention. And then when your grandmother called to berate me some more, she let it slip you were getting married this weekend. I put two and two together and located your father's cell phone. So are you? Getting married? Here?" Mom spoke as if the words tasted bitter in her mouth. As if Las Vegas was the worst place someone could get married. And of course Sarah fell back into a defensive mode.

"What's wrong with here?" The Mighty Grand was a wonderful place. And the chapel was simply beautiful. She couldn't imagine having her wedding at a nicer venue.

"Oh please. Only people who *have* to get married get married here. You're not pregnant, are you?"

Well, at least Dad hadn't spilled the beans to Mom. Apparently he hadn't told her anything. Good. Sarah was done being defensive. Now was the time to attack. "People don't automatically get married because they get pregnant. Sometimes they just don't want to wait. And to answer your other question, John and I are already married. So you can just go back home since there's nothing here for you to ruin."

"Why do you hate me so much? All I ever wanted was for you to have a good life."

"Is that so? What part of raising me did you consider good? Berating me every chance you got? Denying me dinner and eating in front of me because I had the audacity to bring home one B in a fist full of As? Why'd you even have me? Because it sure seemed like I did nothing but make your life miserable."

"Someone had to be the disciplinarian. Your father certainly couldn't do it."

"So you're saying I never did anything right? Because not once did I ever get praise from you. Not once have you ever hugged me."

"Hugging is overrated. And I praised you when you married Steven."

"Which was the worst mistake of my life. How is it you believe him over your own daughter?" Sarah waved her hands. "Never mind. Because there isn't an explanation that will make it better. I just want you out of my life. Do you understand? I don't ever want to see you again. I only want people in my life who make me happy. Who care about my happiness. You do neither."

"You think you can get rid of me that easily? I'm your mother."

"No, you're only the woman who gave birth to me. For that, I'm thankful. Doesn't mean I need to keep you in my life. You don't deserve to be there anyway. So don't bother to come looking for me again. You'll only be wasting your time."

She turned around and nearly ran into John and her father. How long had they been standing there?

"You okay?" John asked.

A nod brought her father forward and he hugged her. "Thanks for allowing me to be a part of your day. I'll get her out of here. You two have fun."

"Are you going to be okay?"

He swiped a finger under her chin. "Never better. I'll call you next week." He held his hand out toward John. "It was good to meet you. Let's not be strangers, okay?"

Clasping her father's hand, John smiled. "You got it."

Guess this was a day for Mom to be manhandled. Dad grabbed her arm and practically dragged her away. "Come on, Carol. It's time we had a talk."

Sarah wrapped an arm around John's waist. "I can't believe I finally told her off. Am I a horrible daughter?"

"No." John kissed the top of her head. "You're a survivor. Now, let's go have some fun. I still owe my bride a dance or two."

Fun. Yeah, dancing with John would be that. "So,

we don't have to go to Atlanta?"

"Nope. Shocking, huh?"

She laughed. Actually, it was the best news ever.

Chapter 11

"Are you sure Barnet's not mad?" Sarah rubbed John's arm, the leather soft under her palm, as they rode up the elevator to their room. "I expected him to stay longer than an hour." If anyone left early, why couldn't it have been Perry?

"He's not mad and I'm sorry I spoiled your recep—"

"Our. Our reception. And you didn't spoil it. That would be Mom. And Perry."

John pulled her in for a hug. "Are you ever going to forgive him?"

Forgive the most egotistical vampire she'd ever met? Probably, because he was John's friend. Didn't mean she wouldn't make him wait, though.

John's scent tantalized her, as it had all afternoon. She wrapped her arms around his neck. "I don't know. Are you going to finish that kiss you started at our wedding?"

"I think I can oblige." He bent down and brought

his lips to hers.

Ah, she could kiss him forever, except the elevator doors opened. She broke the kiss with a sigh, but before she had a chance to depart the elevator, John swooped her into his arms.

"I thought it was customary to carry the bride over the threshold of their home. Not the elevator."

He smiled and headed for their room. "I know you haven't been feeling all that well this afternoon. Plus, I like holding you."

So much for trying to hide her queasiness. Although, maybe there was a cure. She nuzzled her nose alongside his neck and breathed deep. God, that scent. Scrumptious. Calmed her stomach every time. She ran her tongue against his skin and smiled. He tasted as good as he smelled. Maybe even better.

"Mmmm… That feels good. Glad you're feeling better, but you might want to wait until we get inside." He managed to swipe the card and open the door without jerking her at all.

What she had in mind certainly wouldn't work in the hallway. As soon as he shut the door, she bit his neck. Her teeth weren't sharp like his fangs, but she managed to break the skin without much effort. The sweet taste of his blood was exactly what her queasy stomach had been craving.

John moaned and crumpled to his knees, but never dropped her. "Oh God, Sarah. What are you doing?"

"What I've been wanting to do for weeks, now," she said telepathically. His pleasure flowed through their link, as did his arousal. Thank goodness. She'd been afraid he'd get mad, or that she'd hurt him. After a few pulls, the craving vanished. She licked his wound until his healing powers sealed the holes. "Boy, that sure

hit the spot. Thank you, husband."

John stared at her while she sat on his lap. He hadn't tried to stand. He hadn't really moved at all. Had he gone into shock? Or did she have blood on her face? Or worse?

She looked down at her beautiful blouse. "I didn't get any on me, did I?"

"No, you're surprisingly clean." He took her face in his hands. "Sarah, you know I'd do anything for you. Is there something you're not telling me?"

She kissed his lips and smiled. "Think I turned into a vampire?"

"Vampires don't feed from other vampires. Exactly how many weeks have you had this urge?"

He wasn't going to like her answer, but she wasn't about to lie. She stood and walked over to the bed. "Enough to wonder if…maybe…the baby wanted it."

"What? Are you sure?"

She sat on the bed. "Of course I'm not sure. We're a work in progress, right? But let me tell you. That queasiness has disappeared. And I'm not getting the urge to bite you anymore."

He knelt in front of her and frowned. "When you were dancing with Perry, or Barnet, did you get the urge to bite them?"

"Eeeww, no." She couldn't contain the laughter that bubbled out and slapped her hand over her mouth. "I'm sorry. I don't mean to make fun of your worries, but really, the only vampire's blood that was calling to me, or to our baby, was yours. And while you still smell incredible, I only want to consummate our marriage, not bite you. Well, not for blood, anyway."

"What do you suppose it means?" he asked, sitting

back on his heels.

She shrugged. "But I wish you'd stop worrying. I've never felt better." She took his hands. "See for yourself."

He smiled in relief. "You must think I'm a paranoid fool."

"No. I think you love me very much, just as I love you. I promise, if I notice anything wrong, you'll be the first I tell. No more secrets."

"Good. Then maybe next time you get that urge, I can bite a hole on my arm for you. Sure would be a lot easier than biting my neck."

Wow. He was taking this a lot better than she'd expected. She ran her fingers along his healing skin. "There was a time you liked it when I teased you there."

"Because we both thought you'd be a vampire one day."

"Are you saying it doesn't turn you on anymore?" Because she'd certainly gotten the vibe that it had.

"Sweetie, everything you do turns me on."

"Everything?"

He chuckled. "Yeah, everything. And I want to show you how much. Since you're feeling better, I can give you your wedding present now."

"What? I didn't get you anything." She had to be the worst wife ever.

"I didn't get you anything, either, so wipe that frown away." He stood and pointed at her. "Sit there and don't move. Better yet..." He moved the straight-backed chair to the middle of the room and placed her on it.

He withdrew his phone, searched for something, then set it on the night stand. A familiar song played.

Not just any song. "Pony" by Ginuwine. The song Channing Tatum danced to in the movie *Magic Mike*. And now here was John—her John—dancing the same dance. To the same song. For her.

She could barely contain herself.

He slid his leather jacket down his arms and let it fall to the floor. Thrusting his hips, he yanked his T-shirt over his head. Performed a perfect spin and tossed the shirt her way. She caught it on a squeal.

This was the best present ever on the best day ever. God, she loved this man.

* * * *

John moved to the music like that actor had in the movie. He felt like a fool, but Sarah was loving every second of it. Made the time he'd spent practicing worth it.

A few dance steps. Several rolls of his stomach. She squealed when he moved in front of her. As he gave her a lap dance, she reached for him several times, but stopped before any touching was involved. When the roles had been reversed—when she'd basically given him a lap dance—he'd had a hard time not touching.

Oh wait. He'd touched her. All over. Maybe her willpower was stronger.

He unbuttoned his jeans and lowered the zipper, one tooth at a time. Damn, he was getting himself hard. Before he could pop out of his pants, he turned his back on her and shook his hips, lowering the jeans a little at a time.

"Oh, John. You wore a thong? All day?"

His one regret. Should have gone commando. That thing had bugged him to no end. Still, it was a tease and he aimed to tease her. After discarding his jeans, he turned around and undulated his groin within inches of her face. He might have finished the dance if she hadn't yanked the thong free and gone down on his erection.

He let out a groan. Holy sweet, electrifying heat. Guess her willpower wasn't so strong after all. "How is that sitting still?"

She ran her tongue up his glans and released him with a pop. "Sex junkie. Remember?"

Oh, the hell with the dance. "Then get undressed, Mrs. Pennington. Because I aim to consummate this marriage."

"And you can start with feeding from me." She bared her neck while unbuttoning her blouse.

The look of hope on her face brought him to his knees. She wasn't going to like what he had to say. "Sarah, sweetie. I don't think that's wise."

She stopped in mid button. Her pale pink bra peeked out from behind the blouse. Man, he loved the pink one. Oh hell, he loved all her underwear. She was damn sexy in everything. And here he was, spoiling the mood. Why couldn't he have faked it this time and broached the subject later?

"We discussed this. You can't mean not to feed for seven months!"

"Of course not. That would be ridicu—"

"No, no, and no." She grabbed him by the back of his neck. "Don't make me beg."

"But, Sarah. The baby."

"Don't go there. You were feeding from me before you knew I was pregnant."

"And look how weak you were."

"That's only because I couldn't keep any food down. It's different now; I know it."

Maybe it was, maybe her taking his blood made the difference, but how could he be sure?

She cupped his face. "This isn't the same as giving up alcohol or limiting my caffeine intake."

"No, it's your blood."

"Which you don't take much of anyway. Hell, the doctor takes more than you do." Her eyes glistened with unshed tears. It nearly broke his heart. "Please don't do this."

"Sarah, your life, the baby's life, mean more to me than where I feed from. Why is it so important that I only feed from you? You know I'm not going anywhere."

"I know, but I have so few special traits and I like having that one. I like making you stronger. Making you heal faster. And I love the way I feel when you feed from me."

"What do you mean 'few special traits'? Everything you do, everything you are, is special to me."

"You know what I mean. Admit it, you'd feel less paranoid if I were a vampire. A vampire who could do all the amazing things you can."

He ran a hand through his hair. So that's where this was coming from—his paranoia. And here he'd thought he'd hidden it from her. "Sarah, that's not true. My paranoia comes from being a lousy vampire. I holed myself up for over fifty years because I couldn't accept what I had become. If I hadn't done that, I'd be more confident today."

"So you're saying because you're a lousy vampire, you're afraid to feed from me?"

How did she manage to twist his words around? And why did they make sense? "How about a compromise?"

"I'm usually good with those. What do you have in mind?"

"I'll feed from you every other week for two months. If you can handle that without any problems, we can bump it up to every week. But if you so much as wobble on your feet—"

She kissed him on the mouth, silencing his words. "I can live with that. But we'll start the count tonight, right?" When he nodded, she wrapped her arms around his neck. "And just so you know, you're not a lousy vampire. You're the best vampire I know and I'll love you forever, husband."

No more than he loved her and he would do his best to be a better vampire from now on. Because she deserved the best.

Chapter 12

"Don't push," John said.

"That's what you said two days ago, yet that didn't stop me." Sarah wedged in front of John and unbuckled the car seat.

Of course two days ago she'd been giving birth to the most perfect baby ever. Whatever species he ended up being, he'd still taken nearly nine months of growing in her womb before his birth. A birth that capped a rather uneventful pregnancy. After she had taken John's blood, the morning sickness disappeared and never returned.

John was able to continue feeding from her, too, without any adverse effect. It was probably the most boring pregnancy ever. And she couldn't have been more pleased.

Lori came barreling down the back steps of Wings. "Where's little Sean Michael?"

"He's right here." Sarah held her perfect little son, who she'd wrapped in several blankets. "Let's go inside before he freezes."

Lori led the way and as soon as the back door shut, she uncovered the baby's face. "Ohh, look at him. He's adorable." She tore her gaze from Sean and stared at Sarah. "And look at you. You don't look like you had him only two days ago."

Sarah didn't feel like she'd had a baby two days ago, either. Another perk of being a Perfect Mate—no sags, no stretch marks.

"Yes, it is hard to believe," John said as he slid an arm around her shoulders. "But she sure gave me the best birthday present ever, don't you agree?"

"Two handsome men born on January seventh. He doesn't seem premature, does he? And he's got John's eyes, doesn't he, Sarah?"

Sarah nodded. They were blue, she could admit that, but they didn't sparkle like John's. And while Sean had arrived a few weeks early, he was by no means premature. Must have been that vampire blood. Despite her needing John's blood one time, and John's fears their baby would be half-vampire, everything about Sean screamed human. He not only nursed from her, he was able to go out into the sunlight without an issue. John had still tested Sean's blood—her husband needed that scientific proof—and was satisfied with the results. Meant that Sean would probably age while they wouldn't, but she'd worry about that later. She'd given birth to John's son and he was healthy. That was all that mattered right now.

They convened in the bar. Kyle gave Lori a kiss, Sam waved, and Perry glanced up from whatever game he was playing on his phone long enough to smile.

Barnet came over and gazed down at Sean. "You have a fine son, John. A miracle. Truly, a miracle."

The true miracle was that Barnet hadn't required them to live in Atlanta during her pregnancy. He'd been more than satisfied with just getting data from John.

"And you thought your equipment no longer worked," Lori said. "Can I hold him now?"

She didn't even wait for an answer, but took Sean from Sarah's arms like a pro. Then again, she'd had enough practice with her nieces and nephews. As she rocked the baby and sat at a table, she asked, "How's your dad doing?"

Sarah sat with Lori while John talked with the guys. "He's doing well."

She had nearly thrown a party when Dad had called and told her he was moving out. He still hadn't filed for divorce, probably still holding out hope that Mom would change. Sarah wasn't holding her breath on that. "Grandma has been cooking him dinners."

"I swear you have one whacked-out family. But then if I had a daughter like your mom, I might disown her, too. Have you heard from her?"

"Nope." Apparently confronting her mother worked better than any vampire magic.

Kyle sat in the chair beside Lori and kissed her cheek. "Can I hold him?"

"Oh no. Auntie Lori hasn't had him long enough."

Sarah laughed. "You like kids, Kyle?"

"Oh yeah. I have eight nieces and nephews. They're the greatest. I hope to have several of my own."

Lori glanced up at him. "You do? Me, too."

"I knew you were perfect the first moment I met

you." He glanced at Sarah before returning his gaze to Lori. "I had planned this for later, but I can't wait. These past few months have been the best and I'd love to spend the rest of my life with you." Lori's eyes widened when he withdrew a box from his pocket and opened it, displaying one sparkly diamond ring. "Would you do me the honor of becoming my wife?"

"You want me to what?" Lori seemed to come to her senses once Sarah took Sean. She stared at the ring. "Oh my God. Oh my God. Yes. Oh, yes! I'll marry you." After he slid the ring on her finger, she flew into his arms and kissed him.

Sarah carried Sean over to John, giving Lori and Kyle some privacy. She couldn't have been happier for her friend.

Perry slid between them and placed his arms along their shoulders. "Aww, ain't love grand?"

John caressed the baby's cheek and lingered at Sarah's hand. *"He's right, you know? It is grand, and I plan on loving you forever."*

Forever. She liked the sound of that.

BONUS MATERIAL #1

THE LAST CHRISTMAS VISIT

Katarina and Justin are mentioned in *Bite Me, I'm Yours*, *Blind Temptation*, and *A Vampire Wedding*. "The Last Christmas Visit" is the short story of how they met and was originally featured in the anthology *Home for the Holidays*.

THE LAST CHRISTMAS VISIT

Katarina kept her footsteps to a normal pace even though her heart wanted her to run. Passing each decorated house made resisting even harder. All year she waited for Christmas Eve, the one night she risked seeing Michael. Visiting more often was too dangerous.

She turned onto his walkway and came to a halt. Where were the decorations? Where were the lights? Every year Michael had to have the biggest and brightest display and she always teased him about his competitive nature.

Had he finally gotten too old to participate? Did he not want to see her? Disappointment burned in her chest as she continued up the walkway. Low light flickered through the living room window, probably caused by the television. The burn lessened. At least he was up waiting for her.

She pushed the doorbell and stared at the barren yard. The place looked naked – deserted.

The porch light came on and the door opened just

as an idea popped into her head. "Michael, did you need help —?" When she turned around, the words died on her mouth. Those dazzling blue eyes and square jaw were the same, but in a much younger package. "Oh! You're not Michael."

"No. I'm his grandson, Justin. I was expecting Katarina. Are you her granddaughter?"

"No. I'm Katarina." Shoot! In all the years she visited, not once had she encountered his grandson, not even when Justin had moved in fifteen years ago. She had always made sure to arrive after his bedtime.

His eyes widened momentarily. He stood to the side of the doorway and smiled. "Come on in."

When she entered the house, she took in that first wonderful breath. Like coming home, that musky, forest scent enveloped her and set her heart racing. She smiled. All year she waited for that rush. This year was the best yet.

He shut the door against a gust of wind and rubbed his arms. "Where's your coat?"

"It's in the car." Michael knew what she was, so she hadn't bothered to wear it. When Justin looked out at the empty driveway, she continued, "I parked on the street." She bubbled with joy as the tantalizing scent grew stronger, except the living room was empty. "Where's Michael? Did he go to bed already?"

Justin frowned and his eyes glistened. "I'm afraid I have some bad news. My grandfather passed away last month."

What? Michael was dead? Her heart clenched. She knew this day would eventually come. A lot of mortals were lucky to make it to eighty. But why couldn't he live longer?

Justin flipped on a lamp and turned off the TV.

"I'm sorry to be so blunt. Sometimes it's better —"

"No, no. Don't apologize." Her eyes ached with tears she could no longer shed, but her heart was perfectly capable of breaking. She would miss Michael.

"Have a seat." Justin swept a hand toward the couch. "Would you care for something to drink?"

"No, thank you." She numbly sank into the cushion when his earlier statement registered. "You were expecting me."

He sat beside her on the couch and picked up an envelope from the coffee table. "Pops told me you'd come. He wanted me to give you this letter."

Pops. Wow. He'd always been Michael to her, not someone's grandfather. Those extra eighty nine years she had on Michael made her feel downright ancient toward Justin. She took the sealed envelope and went to put it in her purse to read later.

"He asked that you read it now because there's more. But if you'd like me to leave the room…?"

"No, that's okay." It wasn't as if she would burst into tears, no matter how badly her eyes wanted to cry. She opened the envelope and smiled as she ran her fingers over the words. He had hand-written the note. No matter what it said, she would cherish it forever.

My Dearest Kat,

If you're reading this, then you know I have passed on. It is my hope that you will now move on.

Every year I've told you that you didn't need to visit and every year you stubbornly returned. Maybe I should have been sterner. Maybe I should have moved. Somehow, I don't think that would have mattered. You would have found me eventually, of that I am certain.

If I had thought I was the love of your life back in '67, I might have said yes to your proposal. But we both know that I wasn't. I think I was something close to what you were looking for, but for eternity, wouldn't you want the real thing? I know I would.

When my wife died in '65, I really thought it was the end. If not for my children, who knows what I would have done? I certainly didn't expect to ever find love again.

I do love you, Kat, I won't deny it, but not in the way you deserve. And I certainly didn't deserve your yearly visits, although I cherish every one. You made me feel young. For that, I thank you.

I've left you my '63 MG Midget because I know how much you love that car. It just didn't seem right to give it to anyone else. If you decide to keep it, I hope you drive it with joy.

I've had a good life. Really, I have. I don't regret anything. And I've kept your secret, for the most part. I've only told one person, and you're sitting with him. Of course, he didn't believe a word I said, probably thought I was an old man rambling, and maybe I was. But I had to tell him or you would have never received this letter or my gift. It's not like I ever had your address.

When you adjust his memories, as I'm sure you will, please be kind to me. I'd hate to think he will remember me as a raging lunatic.

I wish you a good life, Kat. I hope someday you find that person who lights you up.

Michael

Katarina carefully folded the letter and placed it back into the envelope, then slipped it into her purse. All this time she thought she'd fooled Michael, when maybe she had only been fooling herself. She loved him, but was never in love with him. He seemed to figure that out long before she had. By that time, she'd been hooked on his scent.

But if he had died more than a month ago, his scent should have faded. Why was it stronger than ever? Or could it be…

Nearly thirty years ago she noticed a change. Just a slight difference, but assumed it was Michael. Then fifteen years ago – when Justin moved in after his parents' death – the difference had hit her hard.

Her heart raced. Oh, goodness. It wasn't Michael who drew her here.

Justin produced a set of keys from his pocket. "I believe these belong to you now."

She took the offered keys and stared at his face which was and was not Michael. "You didn't believe your grandfather, did you?"

Justin and Michael shared the same dazzling blue eyes and same sandy-blond hair – before Michael's had turned white – but Justin's lips were fuller and he smelled like…home.

"Believe what?"

"You thought I was Katarina's granddaughter."

"Well, yeah. I guess I just misunderstood. I just can't figure out how long you've known him. You must have been a little—"

"Forty-five years." She smirked at his wide-eyed look. Justin was right about being blunt. Sometimes it was best.

"Forty-five… Then he wasn't lying when he said —"

"I'm a vampire?" She smiled. "No, he didn't lie."

Justin leaned back against the armrest. "Vampires don't exist."

The sounds of his heart racing and blood pumping called to her. Good thing she had fed before coming over, else she might have been tempted to sample him. She wasn't sure she could stop at a taste. "We exist, but we hide well. We have to. But don't worry. I won't bite you."

"You drink blood?"

She hoped the truth wouldn't scare him off. "It's how I live, yes."

"But I didn't see any fangs."

So, he'd looked? Maybe he believed a little, then. Could she get them to extend so soon after feeding? Oh, but he smelled good in that manly way that had nothing to do with food and everything to do with sex. The scent of his arousal synchronized her heart with his. The center of her being clenched. Her fangs extended. *Damn.* That was too easy.

She opened her mouth and acted like it was no big deal. "Convinced now?"

"Wow. That's... Just wow."

That was wow, all right. Why'd he have to be Michael's grandson? She'd probably gross him out if she came on to him. While she could manipulate his mind, she'd rather he liked her on his own and not forced. She fingered the keys as a distraction and her fangs retracted.

"How did you two meet?" he asked.

She relaxed at the change of subject. "The MG broke down. Lucky for him I could fix it. We got to talking, and then one thing led to another."

Justin frowned. The tang of disappointment emanated from him. "You were lovers."

"Does it freak you out, knowing I was with him?" *Please say no.*

"I don't know. Was it recent?"

She laughed. Maybe there was hope yet. "Hardly. He put the kibosh on that in '68."

"And yet you kept on seeing him."

She shrugged. "What can I say. I'm a glutton for punishment."

He scooted closer. "I think you were lonely."

She fought the urge to kiss him, to bury her nose into his neck. "More like hopeful."

"I'm surprised another vampire hasn't snatched you up."

"Most vampires have mates and the man who turned me certainly tried. But Derek thought he owned me and I don't belong to anyone." Too bad Derek didn't see it that way. It had taken her way too much time to slip out this year. No one knew about Michael and she had meant to keep it that way.

"That's nice to hear." Justin's smile lifted her spirits. Maybe this Christmas Eve without Michael wouldn't be so bad after all. If only it could last forever.

They talked for over two hours. She was sure he would want her to leave, but he never gave any indication and she was glad. Even with Michael, she'd never felt so free to be herself.

She stared at the keys in her hand. During their conversation she still hadn't put them in her purse. "Care to go for a drive?"

Oh, but it was too late. He'd never go for it.

He grinned and his striking blue eyes sparkled. "I'd love to."

* * * *

When Katarina smiled, she glowed.

Justin had figured this Christmas Eve would be no

different than the past fifteen. Ever since his parents had died, the holiday held no special meaning. Sure, Pops did his best, but now he was gone, too. So, promising to wait for an old friend didn't spoil his plans whatsoever. It beat watching his cousins whoop it up and revel in a holiday he didn't wish to celebrate.

And that bit about her being a vampire? He had been sure it was the delusion of a senile, old man. But here she sat, looking no older than twenty. How he yeaned to run his hands through her golden blonde hair, feel her creamy white skin, and kiss those to-die-for red lips. Was she putting out some kind of vibe or was she for real?

He thought for sure she would have left by now, but she never gave any indication and he would have discouraged her if she had. Now she wanted to take him for a drive. Could this night get any better?

He stood. "Let me get my coat."

"Is it too cold to put the top down?"

Even in Southern California the nights were chilly, but nothing a coat and the heater couldn't fix. Heck, maybe the cold air would snap him back to reality. He'd been sitting on that couch for the past two hours wondering if he should kiss her. Heck, he'd wanted to kiss her the moment he saw her. "Sounds like fun. Do you need your coat?"

Her heeled boots and jeans – hugging a set of curvy hips – were appropriate for the season, but her halter top – sparkling Christmas red and green – wouldn't have kept anyone warm. Well, anyone human.

"Not really, but it probably would look bad if I wasn't wearing one. I can get it on the way out."

He grabbed his coat and slipped it on. Together

they walked to the garage. He pushed a button, which opened the door and turned on the light. The pale yellow MG Midget stood alongside his Jeep Wrangler.

Just as he reached for the door handle, she did the same and their hands touched. An electric-type current shot through his system and he gasped. Goosebumps formed on his arm. She stared up at him with large eyes. Did she feel it, too?

Neither of them broke the contact and he leaned toward her slightly. Would it really be so bad if he kissed her? Oh, but she would probably think it was gross, having been involved with his grandfather and all.

But that was forty-five years ago. This was now.

She hadn't backed up. In fact, she stared at him with shimmering green eyes, shot a glance to his lips, and smiled.

Oh, the hell with it. He took her face in his hands and planted his lips against hers. She leaned into him and opened her mouth. God, she tasted sweet. She smelled even better. And those fangs of hers? Sexy as hell. He couldn't get enough.

If he didn't get control, he'd take her on the garage floor. That would not do. Not with her. Reluctantly, he broke free.

Her breathing was rapid. "Wow. That's…just wow."

He laughed hearing his own phrase thrown back at him. That kiss was wow all right. He wouldn't mind doing that again. But with them in bed. Naked.

* * * *

If not for the car supporting her, Katarina would have swooned. She'd never been kissed like that. Never felt such warmth. Her lips still tingled and her fangs were still elongated. She usually had better control.

Justin smiled. "I'm sorry if I was a little—"

She cut him off with another kiss. If she thought that first kiss was a doozie, he was definitely better with practice. It took everything in her not to bite him.

"We still going for that car ride?" His voice came out so husky. So low. So sexy.

Oh hell. Was that what they were doing? A car ride would be nice. So would bed. With him. Naked. Maybe the car ride first. Just in case he decided to come to his senses. She'd already spent forty-five years chasing someone who didn't want her. She couldn't do that again. No matter how good he smelled. "You don't mind, do you?"

He opened the driver's door. "I don't mind doing anything with you."

She climbed in behind the wheel and released the top. He pulled it back and secured it before hopping into the passenger seat. The car started right up and she focused on the purr of the engine. She really loved this car.

Justin stroked the dash. "I'm going to miss this car, but I can see why Pops left it to you. You put a lot of love into it, so it was only fitting. Thanks for taking me out for one last ride."

Would it be the last, or maybe the first of many?

She backed out of the garage and Justin closed the door with the remote. Hot and cold did not affect her like they did mortals, so she turned the heater to max. They might be in Southern California, but it was still winter.

She drove the two blocks to her car, where she

had parked next to some woods.

"Why so far away?" he asked.

"A precaution." A silly one, too. Like a vampire couldn't have tracked her down if they wanted. "No one in my… family knew about Michael and I wanted to keep it that way."

"What would have happened if they found out?"

"Erase his memory of me." Probably everything else, too. She couldn't risk Michael's lifetime of memories.

"Erase?" He paused a moment, chewing on his bottom lip. "Is that why he kept the secret?" When she nodded he leaned his head back against the seat. "So, you'll erase my memory?" He turned and stared at her with those same blue eyes that always entranced her, only they didn't belong to Michael now. "That's too bad. I'd like to remember you."

Oh God, she wanted that, and more. But it had to be his choice. No way would she coerce him. "If you'd rather not go for that ride, I'll understand."

"No, I still want to go. Maybe I'll get you to change your mind."

She nearly laughed. Wasn't that what she'd wanted from Michael? And yet, he never had. She pulled the keys to her rental from her purse and was ready to exit when Justin took them from her hand. That little touch sent heat straight to her core.

Mortals shouldn't affect her this way. Her body temperature should match his when touched. But damn, if she didn't love the warmth he sent her way.

"Where is it?"

She blinked like a dumb blonde. Where was what? Oh yes, her coat. "Back seat."

As he hopped out of the two-seater, she exited

more decorously. How else was she going to put her coat on if she didn't stand?

A gust of wind whipped her hair around and brought a familiar scent sending her heart into overdrive. *Shit.*

Derek had found her.

* * * *

Justin leaned inside the back seat and grabbed the blue wool coat.

"Where'd you get the sweet ride, Kitty Kat?"

He froze at the sound of the man's voice. If the guy knew Katarina, he was most likely a vampire. Were all vampires as friendly as her?

"Derek, what are you doing here?" she asked.

"Hey, you don't answer my questions, I figure I'll just follow you and find out on my own."

"Nowhere does it state I have to check in with you twenty-four, seven. I have my own life, you know."

"A life I gave you, if I remember correctly."

Justin pulled out of the vehicle, without her coat. Maybe vampires weren't the threatening creatures of the entertainment industry, but this guy was definitely bugging Katarina. Making him a not-so-nice-guy. Derek was shorter than Justin by a couple of inches and a little thinner. In a normal world, he'd have no problem taking the dude on. Of course his world was no longer normal, was it? Still, he couldn't stand around and watch her get harassed. "Beat it. Can't you tell the lady doesn't want you around?"

He barely blinked when she appeared in front of him. "It's okay, Justin. I can take care of him."

Derek raised his arms into the air. "Ah, shit, Kat. He knows?"

"Go away, Derek. I know what I'm doing."

He approached and stared at Justin. His steely-grey eyes had that same shimmer Katarina's did. Justin stared back. Was this some kind of game? See who blinks first?

"You leave him alone." She yanked Derek's arm away.

Derek broke eye contact with a smug look on his face. He touched her cheek and she shrugged away. "Come on, Kat. Why do you keep fighting me? You know I'm the only one for you."

Justin wedged between the two of them and shoved at Derek's chest. Might as well push a brick wall for all the reaction he got. "Leave her alone. Can't you see she's not interested?"

Derek's eyes nearly popped out of their sockets. He stared at Katarina. "Why did he move? What did you do to him?"

Justin put his hands on his hips. "My feet aren't glued to the ground, now are they?"

Derek's eyes narrowed and his nostrils flared. "Oh, fuck! You fuckin' idiot! Didn't you think to check him first?"

"Hey, that's no way to talk to a lady!"

Katarina grabbed Justin's hand and that electrical jolt surged through him once again. Even she gasped. She looked up at him with sadness in her eyes. "Oh, no." She turned toward Derek. "I don't understand."

"What's not to understand? You told a fuckin' freak, that's what!"

Justin grimaced. He'd been called an ass many times, but never a freak. And he'd never spoken such crude words in front of a lady. "Watch your mouth. She already told me she'd wipe my memory. So what's the big deal?"

"You shut up," Derek said. "I'll say whatever I God-damned want to say."

She stood in front of Justin like some kind of shield. "He's not going to tell anyone, Derek. I'll vouch for him."

So, she wasn't going to wipe his memory? That brought a smile to his face.

"Like hell you will." Derek grabbed her by the throat and lifted her. "You're mine, dammit. I turned you. You'll do as I say."

She clutched his hand and kicked out. "I'm nobody's. Let me go!"

Justin's smile faded. Fear and anger jumbled together and squeezed his heart. What should he do? Could he even fight someone that strong? He searched the area. The branches on the ground were small and would hardly do damage to a squirrel. He picked up the largest he could find, smaller than a pool cue, but maybe enough to distract, when she kicked Derek in the nuts.

The man howled and dropped her on her ass. He grabbed his crotch and fell to his knees.

Well, maybe male vampires weren't all that different than male mortals. Even though Derek deserved it, Justin felt his pain all the same and instinctively reached for his own crotch.

Katarina stood and brushed the leaves from her butt. The kick didn't disable Derek for long, and he lunged at her. She pushed him off and attempted another kick, but he grabbed her leg and swung her around as if she were nothing more than a tetherball. He threw her against a tree.

Her eyes went wide and she cried out. A branch protruded from her shoulder, holding her off the ground at an angle. Blood dripped down her sparkly top.

Derek set his eyes on Justin.

Oh, shit.

If his life had been interesting, he might have seen it flash before his eyes, he was so sure death marched toward him. Would running make him chicken? If so, he might as well start clucking. Only a fool would think he could win a fight against one of them.

But what about Katarina? He couldn't leave her hanging and defenseless.

Derek's stride was slow – maybe he was still sore from that kick – and Justin took the opportunity. He rushed to her and grabbed her waist.

"I'm okay. Just get out of here. The car's still running," she said.

"No doing." He pulled. The force of her release sent him flying backwards. She landed on him with a grunt.

He took in one ragged breath when Derek snatched her by the sparkly top and tossed her aside as if she were a piece of trash. He then grabbed Justin by the coat and yanked him upward.

"Sorry, man, but I can't have you remembering." Derek flashed fangs and slammed Justin to the ground.

Justin wondered if he'd ever suck air again when Katarina skewered Derek with a branch. Blood flowed from where the limb protruded from his chest. His eyes bugged out and he collapsed in a heap. She fell to her knees, clutching her shoulder.

After taking in several wonderful cool breaths, Justin rushed to her side. "Are you okay? Is he dead?"

"No, I'm not dead," Derek grumbled.

"Goddammit, Kat. How could you?"

* * * *

Katarina stared at Derek. The man seriously had no clue.

"What did you do?" Justin asked.

"I pierced his heart, paralyzing him."

"So you don't turn to dust? Or goo?"

"Afraid not." Thank goodness Derek had missed her own heart or she might not have recovered in time to save Justin.

"What's going to happen to him?"

"Good question. He's been told not to harass me any longer. I'll wait until I have some back-up before I let him go." Somehow she would make sure Justin remained safe. "I need to get him into the trunk of my rental before someone comes." She started to stand, but her rubbery legs wouldn't cooperate.

"I can do it." He stood, took two steps toward the car and then stopped. "What if he screams? Won't someone hear?"

"If he knows what's good for him, he'll keep quiet as long as he has that stick in him," she said. Derek was many things, but never stupid when it came to the number one rule of vampires – keep the secret. A rule she apparently needed to learn all over again. Breaking it once was forgivable. Twice? Not so much.

Her shoulder burned and cramps flitted across her stomach. She closed her eyes, lay back on the grass and concentrated on the scents around her. Pine. Grass. Exhaust from the MG. Then the engine died. A new scent appeared. Justin. She opened her eyes.

He knelt beside her. Concern marred his features. "He's secure. Your turn now. What can I do?"

"I'll be fine as soon as I have…" *blood.* She

couldn't say the word. Not to him. No matter how much she needed to feed.

He sat and pulled her into his lap, holding her close. "Does it hurt when you bite? I mean, I assume you need blood. You don't kill to feed, do you?"

She croaked out a laugh that sent shooting pains in her shoulder and stomach. "Yes, I need blood. No, I don't kill. I don't take that much. But as for pain…for normal mortals I can mask it. For you…" She wobbled her head.

"For me? Am I different? Is that why he called me a freak?"

"We can't get into your mind." How did she miss all the signs? His tantalizing scent. The rush of warmth from his touch. If she had only tried to read him earlier, maybe they wouldn't be in this mess.

He paused for a moment and then his eyes widened. "Oh. So you couldn't erase my memory even if you wanted?"

"I don't want to, but, no." Damn, he smelled good. His closeness caused her fangs to extend. Too bad it had nothing to do with feeding.

He lifted her so her mouth was beside his neck. "I assume the neck is best?"

"I can't ask…"

"You're not asking. I'm offering. Just be quick, okay? If you must know, I'm kind of a baby when it comes to pain."

Offering? She pushed on his chest and he lowered her. "Justin, because I can't get into your mind, if you offer me your blood, there's a good chance we'll be bonded."

"Is that a good thing, or a bad, slave-like thing?"

She smiled. "It's a good thing between two people

in love. But you hardly know me. A bond is forever."

He ran his fingers through her hair, brushing it in a soft, gentle stroke while he stared into her eyes. "What about you? What do you want?"

She wanted to love this man and was fairly sure she could. "I have to do what is right for you. What I want doesn't matter."

He frowned. "Of course it matters. We decide together, okay? So, this is how I see it. You can't wipe my memory. And if the other vampires are like your maker, then I'm guessing my life is pretty much in danger. Would I be correct in that assumption?"

"Probably, but I wouldn't let—"

He put a finger to her mouth. "Would this bond save me?"

She wished it would. "I don't know. Being turned would, though."

"You can do that? You can turn me?"

"Not without permission from my… family. But that's only a formality, to make sure you're okay with it. Do you really want to be a vampire?"

He kissed her lightly on the lips sending warmth throughout her body. "I'll do whatever it takes to stay alive. And be with you. But only if you want me."

She smiled. "I'd be honored to ask for permission."

He lifted her to his neck. "Good. Now feed already."

He made sense to her addled mind. And he wanted to be a vampire; she didn't have to ask. She sat up to situate herself just right and then sunk her fangs into his neck. The wonderful coppery flavor rolled across her tongue, the best she'd ever tasted.

His blood took away the pain and gave her

strength. It also awakened her body. If only they were naked.

As she drank, he panted and squeezed her tight. If she didn't stop now, she might never let go. He shuddered and cried out. She removed her fangs and licked the site, healing her marks. Was he okay? Had she hurt him?

He grabbed her face and kissed her as if he were staking a claim. She'd never wanted anyone more.

"Damn," he said. "If that's a bond, I'll take it. How are you feeling?"

She lifted her shoulder with ease. "Great."

He brushed his lips against hers. "Thank you."

"For what?" He'd healed her, and rather quick, too. She should be thanking him.

"For walking into my life. Immortality with you will be the best Christmas gift I've ever been given."

She touched the face of this man who she would love. Except he got it all backwards. He was her gift. This was her last Christmas visit. She was home.

BONUS MATERIAL #2

FOREVER THIRTY-TWO

John Pennington's origin story is told in the short story "Forever Thirty-Two," which is available free in digital. This is the first time it's been in print.

FOREVER THIRTY-TWO

"Ahhh!" Mrs. Randolph cried over the cheers of "Happy New Year" in the hallway.

"Her husband's not going to be happy," Noreen muttered as nineteen fifty-six turned into nineteen fifty-seven.

John shot the nurse a quick glance and understood her concern, but at the moment he was a little busy. "You're doing fine, Mrs. Randolph. I need you to push again."

Twenty minutes later and still no baby, and she'd been pushing for over an hour. The tyke hadn't been in any hurry to arrive and John wasn't about to rush it. Sometimes it was like that. But while other doctors drugged their patients during birthing, John believed in keeping them awake. He'd discovered the mothers were happier that way, too. Although at the moment, Mrs. Randolph might not agree with that.

He cradled the head as it crowned. "Great job. This is it. I have its head. One more push."

Her face turned red and the cords on her neck

popped, but that last push worked. Offering encouragement to the mother, John guided the infant as it emerged into the world.

"It's a boy," he said over the baby's cries.

"Oh, thank God," Mrs. Randolph sobbed.

John placed the infant on the mother's towel-covered stomach and clamped the cord. He wrapped the infant.

Tears ran down her cheeks as she tentatively touched her son. "He's okay?"

"He's doing just fine. We'll cut the cord in a bit and then clean him up." He glanced at the clock and spoke quietly to Noreen. "Time of birth: twelve twenty-seven a.m."

The nurse smirked as she wrote down the information.

"Don't worry. Once he sees his son, it'll be all right."

"Whatever you say, Doctor."

* * * *

Smoke engulfed the waiting area and John nearly choked on the fumes. He'd voiced his opinion regarding the hospital and smoking, but he might as well have spoken to the damn cigarettes with the results he'd achieved. It just didn't seem right to allow something that dirty in an environment they wanted clean.

With a cigarette dangling from his mouth, Mr. Randolph stood when he saw John. Ash from the tip sprinkled down the front of his shirt. "Well, Doc?"

"Congratulations, Mr. Randolph," John said as he extended his hand. "You have yourself a son."

Mr. Randolph pulled the cigarette from his mouth, his eyes bugged out. "It's a boy? It's a boy?" He grinned from ear to ear and slapped his leg, ignoring John's hand. "Hot damn. I didn't think she had it in her. Did he arrive before midnight?"

John pulled his hand back. "I'm afraid not. He was a little stubborn and didn't want to leave his home. He arrived after midnight."

Mr. Randolph's face scrunched up in anger. He turned away and kicked the closest chair to him. It clattered on its way to the wall. "Damn her. She can't do nothing right. If she had just had the baby when she was due, but nooooo. Not her. The bitch."

John seethed as he righted the chair. He'd never been tempted to strike someone, but then he'd never met anyone like Mr. Randolph, either. "Why is it so important to you? I can't imagine the tax deduction—"

"Taxes? She screwed up my taxes, too?"

"Your taxes are fine, Mr. Randolph, but if that wasn't your concern, what is?"

The man lowered his head and kicked at the ash that had landed on the floor. "Well, I might have had a little bet going on." He looked up with hope in his eyes. "You sure you couldn't fudge the time?"

All this over a stupid bet? The idiot deserved to lose. "I'm sorry, but I must follow hospital rules." Before he could get into an argument, Noreen stood on the other side of the glass, holding the baby.

Now there was something that would change Mr. Randolph's attitude.

"Would you like to see your son? He's just over there." John motioned to the window.

"Yeah, sure." Mr. Randolph stabbed his cigarette in the overflowing ashtray and flinched when he saw the boy. "What's the matter with him? He's all wrinkly."

John chuckled, trying to get the man to loosen up. "All newborns look like that, Mr. Randolph. There's nothing wrong with him. He's healthy and strong. In a few days his skin will—"

"He's ugly," Mr. Randolph wailed. "She can't even birth a handsome baby. Now I got an ugly son born in the wrong year." He walked over to the nearest chair and plopped himself down. "Wait'll I see her. She'll get a piece of my mind." He then looked up at John. "So, Doc, when can I see her?"

Certainly not tonight. Mrs. Randolph didn't deserve to be berated after all her hard work and Mr. Randolph needed time to think things through, so John lied. "It would be best to wait until morning. She's had a rough night and needs her rest. I'm sure a good night's sleep will make you feel better, too."

"I doubt that," he said, as he stood and shuffled out of the waiting room.

* * * *

By one-thirty, John was beat. After placing his hat upon his head, he reached for the exit.

"Dr. Pennington, wait up."

He stopped and turned around. "What can I do for you, Noreen?"

She trotted up to him, as if she were afraid he'd walk out before she had a chance to talk. A little out of breath, she said, "I just wanted to thank you."

"Thank me? For what?"

"For making Mr. Randolph leave. Mrs. Randolph broke down after you left when she realized what year the baby was born in. She seemed truly scared to see her husband."

"Oh, he'll calm down once he's had a good night's

sleep. Who wouldn't be happy to have a son?"

"I hope you're right." She tugged on the hem of her sweater and chewed on her bottom lip.

"What else ails you?"

"Why couldn't you just write down that the baby was born before midnight?"

John sighed. He'd wondered when she'd get around to asking. And while he had lied to Mr. Randolph about hospital rules, and not just because of the bet, Noreen could handle the truth. "That baby chose his birthday, not me. I'm not about to go against his wishes."

"Is that what you really think?"

"Don't you?"

She smiled. "I do now. Happy New Year, Doctor."

"Happy New Year to you, too, Noreen."

John opened the door to falling snowflakes. Nineteen fifty-seven was already looking to be a good year. He hoped it snowed heavy and long. He loved the way the world looked after a good snow. Clean and pure.

He buttoned up his coat and wrapped his scarf around his neck. As he walked through the park toward his apartment, he thought about Mr. Randolph's reaction to his son. If John were to be a father, he'd be jumping for joy. He loved kids. But with the hours he kept, would he ever find anyone to spend his life with, have children with? He'd come close once, but that was before med school and she'd ended up breaking it off after meeting her soul mate. John couldn't fault her for that.

"Where are you off to in such a hurry, gorgeous?" a woman said from behind.

He skidded to a stop. Damn, he'd never even heard anyone approach. He turned around and became dazzled by her loveliness. Her coat was open revealing a red dress that clung to her body like a second skin. Wavy blonde hair cascaded down to her tiny waist. She was curvy in all the right places, but John was drawn to her eyes. An icy blue, they mesmerized him.

He blinked a couple of times to clear his head. Was she a hooker? While he was sure they existed in Columbus, Ohio, he'd never run into one before. But who else would be out this time of night alone? "I'm sorry, miss, but I'm not interested."

Don't leave.

What was that? He would have left, but he had to stay. It was important he stayed.

She strolled up to him and ran her hand down his arm. "I don't know whether I should be flattered or insulted. But I'm not a prostitute, if that's what you're worried about. I happened to see you walk past and decided I wanted to get to know you better. Can you blame me? Has anyone told you how handsome you are?"

John had been told, but it wasn't anything he dwelled upon. His looks were his looks. He couldn't help the kind of genes his parents handed him. "Whatever you're offering, I'm not interested."

"Ah, don't be that way." She took his hand. She wasn't wearing any gloves and for a moment they were cold—almost as cold as the air—but his hand warmed hers up quickly.

Invite me over, John.

Again, that voice tickled his mind. Had she spoken to him or was his conscience telling him something?

Well, he couldn't leave her out in the cold. "You're freezing. Why don't you come home with me and warm up?"

"Why, thank you, John. I'd love to." She slipped her arm through his and rested her head on his bicep. "Lead the way."

"How do you know my name? Do I know you?"

When she looked up at him with those dazzling eyes, blood rushed straight to his groin. "Aren't you Dr. Pennington? Deliverer of babies?"

He relaxed even while his erection remained. "Yes, I guess you could say it like that, but you aren't one of my patients."

"No, you're right. I'm not. Doesn't mean I'm not interested in you. My name is Danielle and my greatest hope is that we get to know each other better."

Yes. He wanted that, too. Smiling, he squeezed her arm affectionately as they walked through the park. Taking her home felt right. As if she were the one he'd been searching for his whole life.

* * * *

For the next several nights, John spent his free time with Danielle. The more time he spent with her, the more he wanted her. She was all he dreamed about. He'd be with her all day long if he could, but she'd either show up at his doorstep shortly after sundown or meet him at the hospital on the nights he worked late. When he'd offered to pick her up at her place or suggested they meet for lunch, she'd always declined. Had said she wanted to keep some things a mystery.

She was a mystery, all right. One he wanted to solve. No woman had ever consumed him like she had.

On the night of January seventh, John sat at home, waiting for Danielle. His last patient had left at four, so on his walk home he'd stopped and bought a bottle of wine, a block of cheese, and crackers. Danielle had never eaten during her visits—she'd always arrived claiming she wasn't hungry—but maybe she would enjoy the appetizers. It was his birthday and he wished to celebrate.

And maybe after the appetizers, he and Danielle could be the main course.

She must want him. The last six nights she'd teased him to no end, snuggling and kissing—spending extra time at his neck—with some heavy petting, until he'd nearly come in his pants. One time he could have sworn she'd left him a hickey of some sort, but his neck never showed any sign.

Every night he'd waited for her to ask for more, but she never had. Maybe he'd been going about it all wrong. He wanted her in his bed. To make love to her. To spend the night. So he would ask her tonight.

A little after five-thirty, a knock sounded on his door. John opened it to Danielle. Such radiance. She wore a clingy blue dress cut so low it almost exposed her areolas. The heels on her shoes were at least four inches tall, and he still had to bend over to kiss her lips.

And her lips were so soft and yielding. If he didn't watch it, he'd take her on the floor, which wouldn't benefit the seduction he had planned. He pulled back. "I've missed you."

"I've missed you too, dear," she said, caressing his arm. She brushed against his growing arousal as she entered his apartment. "So what is all this?"

He slipped off her coat and hung it in the closet. "I bought some cheese and crackers and wine. I thought we could celebrate. You see, today is my birthday."

She clasped her hands together. "It is? Well then, Happy Birthday, John. How old?"

"Thirty-two."

"What a perfect age. I wish I had known sooner. I would have bought you something."

He led her to the couch and sat beside her once she adjusted her dress. "I don't need anything. Well…except maybe you."

"Aren't you the sweetest thing?"

Kiss me, John.

That voice in his head returned and an uncontrollable urge came over him. He leaned into her and kissed her hard. Her mouth was like candy and he couldn't get enough. On top of that, her flowery scent drove him wild.

She grabbed his crotch and he nearly exploded. "I think I've been making you wait too long, huh, John? Maybe that can be my present to you."

"I don't want to force you to do anything you're not ready for, Danielle. But I do want you. More than anything."

"Do you love me John?"

Tell me you love me.

"Yes," he said, kissing her neck. "I love you and I want to make love to you." He slipped his hand inside her dress and caressed her breast—she wasn't wearing a bra or slip of any kind and it got him hotter. Her nipple was hard and he wanted to taste it, but she held his face in her hands and pulled him away.

"I love you, too, John. I knew it from the first

moment I laid eyes on you. We could be together forever, you know? I want you forever, John."

"Forever? As in marriage? Are you proposing, Danielle?" He could marry her. He could marry her in a heartbeat. Hell, he should have asked her first. Was that what she'd been waiting for?

She stood and let her dress fall to the ground. She wasn't even wearing panties. On unsteady legs, he managed to rise and face her. After tugging his shirt free, she unbuttoned it and slipped it off his shoulders, running her hands over his chest and causing his own nipples to harden. She unbuckled his belt while he slipped off his shoes. As she lowered the zipper to his pants, she softly caressed his groin. Pleasure shot through him and he moaned. He'd never been so turned on before.

"My my, John. You're a surprise all around, aren't you? I don't think I've ever had anyone as large as you. You must really pleasure the women, huh?"

He'd never had any complaints in that department. It was usually his schedule his dates had objected to.

"But to answer your question," she said, "no, I'm not proposing marriage. I'm proposing something better."

Better than marriage? "I want more than just sex with you."

"I know you do, dear. It will be more than just sex. So much more."

After removing his slacks and socks, she pushed him down to the couch and straddled him. "You really are one gorgeous man, you know that, John? I'm surprised someone hasn't snatched you up. I'm just glad I found you before you were."

He was glad, too. He couldn't imagine his life

without her. But the couch was no place to do what he wanted to do to her. He grabbed her by the butt and stood.

"Where are we going?" she asked.

"My bedroom. It'll be more comfortable there."

She wrapped her legs around his waist. "Then take me there."

She wasn't too heavy, but she still wore her shoes and the heels dug into his hips. When he reached the bed, they collapsed onto the soft mattress.

"So what's better than marriage and more than just sex?" he asked.

"That, my dear, will be your present. First, I want you to love me. Love me like you never loved another."

He pulled a condom from his nightstand, but she tossed it back. "We won't be needing that."

He would have argued—babies should come after marriage—but that voice in his head told him not to worry, so he didn't. After climbing on top of her, he kissed her deep and caressed her breast, playing with the taut nipple. She gripped his penis, guiding him. Not needing another hint, he slowly entered her. His size was usually too large for most women to take quickly. Slow and steady caused the least amount of pain.

Danielle arched up to meet him. "Hard and fast, John. I can take it."

He'd never done it like that, couldn't imagine any woman enjoying it that way, but that voice inside him urged him on. He thrust into her and she moaned in ecstasy.

She was tight, but wet, and he was able to move in and out with ease. He gave it to her hard, pushing her into the mattress. Pressure built, but he held back, wanting her to come first.

She sucked his neck and moaned. "One last taste, my dear."

What had she meant by that? He felt a prick where her mouth was. God, was she biting him? The sensation got him hotter; he thrust faster.

She moaned as she came, clawing at his back. Sweet Jesus, she tightened up, and it took him over the edge. As he came inside her, she kissed his cheek. "Happy Birthday, John. I love you."

Tell me you love me, that you want to be with me forever.

"I love you, Danielle. I want to be with you forever," he said.

"Here's my present. We'll be together forever, now."

She bit down on his neck. Burning pain streaked through his veins, as if he'd been injected with poison. From her bite, down his arms, through his chest down to his legs—his whole body was an inferno. He screamed. "What did you do to me?"

She rolled him on his back and held his face in her hands. "I'm sorry, darling. Soon you won't feel anything, though. I promise."

She was so wrong. He felt something. One thing. Unending, unbearable pain.

At one point she dressed him in slacks and a T-shirt. He had no idea when that occurred or how long he'd been laying there—the minutes felt like hours and the hours felt like days. As he lay there suffering, Danielle covered his windows with foil. Why would she do that? But he was so far gone, he wasn't sure if he'd asked her or if she'd answered. The pain ate at him. If he endured it much longer, he would go mad.

"Please kill me, Danielle. I can't take this anymore."

"I'm sorry, John. I really didn't think the venom would take this long. If I could control the pain, I would. Please bear with it a little longer, darling. You will feel better soon. I promise."

Her idea of soon didn't come soon enough, but eventually the burn subsided. However, a different kind of pain replaced it. His stomach twisted in a cramp. "Now what? What's wrong with my stomach?"

"You're only hungry, John. But it's not night, yet. We can't go out until then."

"What do you mean? What are you talking about?" She wasn't making any sense whatsoever.

She smiled at him. "You're a vampire, John. Like me. You'll be thirty-two forever."

A vampire? She was insane, that's what she was. John moved to the edge of the bed, but the cramps hit him hard and he flopped back on the mattress. "I need a doctor. You gave me poison or something."

"No poison. Only venom. My bite did this to you, John. Please don't fight it. The sun will set soon. Then we'll go out and feed."

"You're crazy, you know that? Just stay away from me." When he looked at Danielle, really examined her, the dazzling woman he'd first met was gone. Her hair was still blonde and wavy, but lacked the brightness he'd noticed before. Her eyes were still an icy blue, but had lost their vibrancy. Instead, they were flat and practically blended in with the whites of her eyes. Her body was still curvy, but her age showed. Where he'd thought she might be in her twenties, it seemed he needed to add a decade.

The most astonishing reality: he wasn't in love with her. Had he ever been?

"John, don't say that. I love you. Once you feed, you'll feel better. I promise."

"Stop promising," he yelled. "Just leave."

She reached out to touch him, but he pulled back, causing another cramp. Every time he moved, it hurt.

"Get out," he yelled. "Get out of my home and never come back."

"Oh dear," she said. "What am I going to do?" She went into the living room, picked up the phone, and dialed one long digit, most likely the operator. He couldn't see her, but the sounds were so crisp and clear, he might as well be standing right beside her. "I need to make a long distance call to Atlanta." She gave the operator a number.

Who the hell was she calling in Atlanta? And how could they help him up here in Columbus? He'd probably be dead before anyone could arrive anyway.

"This is Danielle. I need to speak to Barnet. What do you mean 'Danielle who?' Delaveaux, you imbecile."

Seemed someone possessed a short temper. He'd laugh if he had it in him. What had he ever seen in her? And how had he missed how crazy she was?

Or was he the one who was crazy? With the windows covered and no lamp lit, the room should have been pitch black. Instead, he could make out the furniture and the walls and the ceiling. Where was the light coming from?

And what was with his hearing? Not only had Danielle's movements been crystal clear, but a couple argued as if they were in John's room. When he moved his head around, he discovered the conversation was happening upstairs. How was that possible? And how could he shut it off?

"Barnet, I need some help," Danielle said. "I might have screwed up."

* * * *

"Screwed up" had been an understatement. By the time her help arrived, John was curled in a corner, too weak to move, having refused any help Danielle offered. As if his neighbor, who had seemed catatonic at the time, could have been any help at all. Danielle had spoken crazy talk again, claiming his fangs would emerge if he'd only sniff the man. It had gotten best to just ignore her.

An older man approached John. "Son, my name is Barnet. I'm so sorry. What Danielle did to you was wrong, but I'm here to help." He continued explaining exactly what it was that she had done. And he couldn't apologize enough.

Seemed Danielle wasn't completely crazy. And she hadn't lied. John was a vampire and he would be thirty-two forever. He could never go back to his job, or see his family. She'd taken everything away from him and he hated her. For the next several months, John learned what it was to be a vampire and how to survive among the mortals. The only good news he'd received during that time was hearing that Danielle had been sentenced to death.

Seemed even vampires had their rules. And the newest one involved illegal turnings. A vampire was required to get the permission from the mortal, as well as the Committee, before the mortal could be turned. Danielle had done neither. She'd claimed she'd gotten John's consent, but the proof in John's memories had been all the Committee needed: she'd controlled him from the start. He hadn't witnessed her death, but was happy it had occurred, and that alone tore him up inside.

John learned to feed, to take blood from humans. It was something that took awhile for him to get used to. Being a doctor, it seemed wrong. But once he'd been shown that vampires never took enough to cause any damage, it became tolerable.

In May, and with his new-found mental abilities, John visited Columbus—the last time for several decades. There was one last thing he wanted to do before he moved on with his new life.

He walked up to Apartment B and knocked.

Mrs. Randolph opened the door. "Dr. Pennington? What are you doing here? I heard you were missing."

He slipped into her mind. *"You never saw Dr. Pennington. Call your husband, then go into the living room and watch TV."*

Her eyes glazed over. "Ernie, there's someone at the door for you." She shuffled toward the living room.

One of these days he would figure out how to control a mortal without them looking like a zombie. His new friend, Perry, had said it would take practice.

"What the hell's the matter with you?" Ernie Randolph said to his wife as he stumbled into the entryway. In four months time, the man had become a bigger mess. Stains ran down the front of his sleeveless undershirt and the holes in his pants exposed his knees. Smoke trailed behind him as another damn cigarette dangled from his mouth.

Before John let the man utter another word, he slipped into Ernie's mind. *"You will treat your wife with love and tenderness. You will love your son with adoration. You will no longer smoke or gamble and will take care of your appearance. And you will do it all with joy. Forever. That is an order.”*

"Goodbye, Mr. Randolph. Enjoy your son."

ABOUT THE AUTHOR

Stacy McKitrick always had stories in her head; she just never knew what to do with them. Then one day she decided to give writing a try and discovered the passion she'd been looking for all her life. She waived goodbye to accounting and now spends her time writing romance featuring vampires and ghosts. All with happy endings, of course. Born in California, she currently resides in Ohio with her husband. They have two grown children.

If you'd like to be kept updated on the latest news and releases, please sign up for her newsletter at http://eepurl.com/-Auwz.

Want more? Stop by her website at http://stacymckitrick.com for excerpts and buy links to all her books.

9 780996 797634